UNICORN TRACKS

Julia Ember

Harmony Ink

Published by
HARMONY INK PRESS

5032 Capital Circle SW, Suite 2, PMB# 279, Tallahassee, FL 32305-7886 USA
publisher@harmonyinkpress.com • harmonyinkpress.com

Unicorn Tracks
© 2016 Julia Ember.

Cover Art
© 2016 Meghan Moss.
http://meaghz.deviantart.com/gallery/
Cover content is for illustrative purposes only and any person depicted on the cover is a model.

ISBN: 978-1-63476-878-8
Digital ISBN: 978-1-63476-879-5
Library of Congress Control Number: 2015914165
Published Edition April 2016
v. 1.0

Printed in the United States of America
∞
This paper meets the requirements of
ANSI/NISO Z39.48-1992 (Permanence of Paper).

For the family members, friends, and teachers who read the stories, novel attempts, and bad fan fiction that I wrote as a child and encouraged me to just keep trying.

Chapter One

MUDDY WATER filled a paw print the depth and width of a soup bowl. I knelt on the red earth, brushing aside leaves and debris. The tracks led from the edge of the path into the brush. A sinuous channel left by the creature's serpentine tail wound in and out of the prints.

I bit my lip to hide a grin of triumph. Nobody at the camp had spotted a chimera in months. If I managed to find one of the elusive beasts, the other guides would finally have to stop saying that Tumelo only hired me because I was his cousin. Even Oswe would have to admit that a girl tracker had bested him. I almost rubbed my hands with glee, imagining the look on his face. Crawling forward, I used the butt of my rifle to separate the dense bushes like thorny curtains. A steaming pile of manure greeted me, and I sat up, pinched my nose, and wiped red sand on my breeches. We were close.

"What is it, Mnemba?" One of my tourists leaned forward in her saddle to peer down at the ground, adjusting her sweat-soaked skirts. "A lion?"

I shook my head, tracing the twisting line with my finger. "No, see this long mark? It's a chimera. The snake tail drags behind."

"A *chimera*, Suzette!" Her husband clapped his hands together. "Mary Ellis told me that when they went on safari—"

I cut him off, mounted up again, and wheeled my horse abruptly off the path. In the three days since I became the Dyers' guide, I'd heard more than enough stories about "Mary Ellis" and her Nazwimbe adventures. My mare, Elikia, snorted, showing the disdain I felt.

"Stick close behind me," I instructed, nudging Elikia straight through the knee-high ferns. "We're near, and the chimera might be hunting. Follow the trail I make with my horse."

"What do they eat?"

"Anything. Just keep the noise down. We don't want to startle it."

"Paul was first regiment. He'll protect us," Suzette said, patting her husband's shoulder proudly. The newlywed Dyers exchanged sickly sweet smiles.

Paul Dyer pulled his rifle over his shoulder and cocked it. His finger hovered over the trigger, and he took mock aim at a tree behind us. A phoenix chattered up in the tree's heights, preening its magnificent orange and red feathers.

"Right," I said, trying not to roll my eyes. "Just stay quiet so I can concentrate."

I scanned the earth, looking for snapped branches and flattened grass. Once off the path, the plants grew too thick for me to see the chimera's tracks from horseback, but I didn't dare dismount again. If we stumbled upon the creature, the last place I wanted to be was on the ground. Elikia trudged through the thick foliage, shaking her head as mosquitos buzzed around her nostrils. Behind me, the Dyers swatted at insects on each other's backs.

A deep rumble shook the ground beneath our horses' hooves. My heart froze, and I turned in my saddle to face a moss-covered outcrop. Staring down at us from above, the chimera licked her front paws and stretched out in the sun, enormous belly bulging with meat. Her snake-headed tail continued to feed as she rested, gulping down dark strips of red and gray flesh from the tattered elephant carcass lying beside her.

A few hundred feet away, the elephant's herd milled about in the trees, sadly waiting to venerate their friend's skeleton once the huge cat had finished her meal.

"Where's my sketchbook?" Suzette whispered to her husband. "Can you get it out of your saddlebag?"

I shook my head at Paul before he could climb down. As much as I would have loved to shove a drawing of the chimera in Oswe's smug face, the last thing we needed was to pique the creature's interest by dismounting.

Paul's horse stamped at the ground, trying to the shake the bugs off his legs.

The chimera's purple eyes snapped open. Her pupils dilated with interest, and she sniffed at the air. The snake tail hissed and a low, rocky growl formed in the great cat's throat. Her lips parted, revealing yellow, stained canines each the length of my index finger.

"Everyone stay still," I said, keeping my voice as calm as I could.

"Stay still? Are you insane?" Paul Dyer fumbled with his rifle, struggling to brace it. His fingers slipped on the trigger, and the gun's barrel shook.

The chimera climbed to her feet, staring at us. She crouched low on her haunches and positioned herself to pounce.

I looked around, frantically searching for a way to escape without having to shoot the magnificent creature. As a guide, my first duty was to protect our guests from harm, but how could I shoot something so rare it had almost melted into legend?

Two young bull elephants sparred in the trees, tusks locking together. I whipped my rifle over my shoulder and shot the ground under their feet. The noise spooked the already edgy herd. They trumpeted in alarm, ears fanning as they stampeded. The chimera's head twisted toward the movement. Looking between the elephants and her half-devoured prey, she tucked her tail, leapt down from the cliff, and sought refuge in the caves below.

I let out a sigh of relief. The Dyers' pale skins had taken a greenish tinge with fright. A tuft of the chimera's mane stuck to the rocks above us. Pins of adrenaline made my fingers tremble as I stood in my stirrups, untangling the silky hair and hiding it in my saddlebag.

I slowly turned Elikia back toward the path, intent on finding a creature my tourists could approach with a little less danger.

"I HAVE a gift for you, Mnemba," Tumelo called out to me as I passed the wooden shack he used as an office. He sat with his bare feet up on his desk, puffing deeply on a luxury cigar one of the tourists had given him as a parting gift. Smoke billowed out toward me. He beckoned me with the crook of his finger. "Come in."

I stumbled over to the hut on tired legs and sat in the chair opposite him, helping myself to a mango from his bowl of fruit. Tumelo's "gifts" weren't always things I appreciated—a frightened new horse to train up, breakfast shifts so early the sun hadn't even thought about coming up—so I helped myself to other little things from him to make up for it. I'd grown up bouncing in the saddle behind him, poking him in the ribs, trying to make him fall, so I felt more at ease with him than some of the other guides did.

Rolling my eyes, I braced myself. "What is it?"

He brandished an open envelope, with a thick letter crumpled and stuffed back inside. Like everything else he owned, the white paper was smeared with tobacco dust. Tumelo beamed. "A naturalist from Echalend is visiting us here for field research. And I have decided to assign him to you."

"A naturalist?" I dug my safari knife into the mango's tough skin. "For what? And why would I want one?"

"You're always complaining your guests don't know enough and almost get killed. Well, now's your chance to show an expert around."

"Then he'll know too much!" I protested. How could I work my usual strategies with a bona fide nature expert? He would know the difference between the hoof prints of a wildebeest and an abada. And he definitely wouldn't believe that a nightingale was a baby caladrius. On days when I couldn't find the tracks of the beasts the

4

tourists paid big money to come and see, I relied on those tricks to keep them happy and believing in my skills. "Why can't you ever give me a good present? Like a pair of riding gloves or a new rug for my hut or something?"

"Never satisfied." Tumelo heaved a dramatic sigh, but he was smiling. "Well, it doesn't matter. Mr. Harving and his daughter will be here within the day. They wrote to me from Ekwaga a few days ago."

"So, you're saying I have no choice? Send Oswe, he's itching for a challenge." Since I'd found the chimera two days before and presented her hair to the entire camp as proof, Oswe had stomped about in a huff, avoiding all eye contact with me. Victory was sweet.

"When you're not being a lazy cow, you're my best tracker, so if anyone can find whatever it is they want to study, you can."

"If I'm your best, you should treat me with more respect."

"As a person, I respect you loads. But I can't always respect your wishes. If I did, we'd be out of business."

I stuck my tongue out at him.

"You'd better wash up, braid your hair, and get ready to receive them."

"Today's my day off. I haven't had a day off in weeks. I'm totally burned out," I grumbled, biting into the fruit. A trail of juice trickled down my chin.

The Dyers had left that morning, bursting with stories of animal sightings to tell their friends at home. As exhausting as they had been, at least the scatterbrained couple had left me much better presents than the one Tumelo offered now. The bar of white chocolate from their home in Frecklin called to me from my hut. I could almost feel the ghost of its creamy sweetness melting on my tongue. Chocolate was rare here and expensive. It almost made putting up with them worth it.

Suzette had also given me a beautiful woven dress from the market they explored on an excursion to town. I would wear it the next time I visited home. Whenever I got up the courage.

"You can have four days off after they leave," Tumelo said, handing me another mango from his cracked bowl. "Time enough to be a dutiful daughter and go home to see your mama. She keeps writing me letters about you. She said if you don't come home to celebrate your seventeenth birthday with them, I'm to deliver you—slung over a pack mule."

"You'd never do that."

"I would so. I bet they'd even pay me for your safe delivery."

I sighed, pocketing the second mango for later. He *would* do it, especially if money was involved. Mama always wrote directly to him, knowing I wouldn't tell her the truth of how I was. My hand traveled to my stomach, hovering over the scars hidden by my linen shirt. "You know why I don't go back."

Tumelo drew a long breath from his cigar, taking in the smoke as greedily as a drowning man getting his first gulp of fresh air. "You can't avoid home forever. What happened wasn't our family's fault. Don't punish them for it."

I nodded, my back stiffening. Changing the subject to something that didn't hurt quite so much, I pointed my finger at him. "Fine, I'll get ready for the new guests, but I want those four days off, even if all I do with them is bum around here. Doesn't matter how lazy I'm being; you don't get to ask me to do anything. No exercise rides, kitchen shifts, nothing. Deal?"

"Deal," Tumelo agreed. He spat in his palm, and we shook on it.

I picked up the rest of his fruit bowl, winking. "And this. I'm taking this back to my hut to enjoy."

Tumelo just laughed. His hand bounced on his great belly as it rumbled.

I WAS still submerged up to my chin in water, with a white, sugary moustache, when Bi Trembla, the camp's housekeeper, burst through the mpacasa-hide flap into my hut. I popped the last of the chocolate into my mouth, peering guiltily up at her through wet lashes.

She put both hands on her hips, her lips quirking sternly when she glanced down at me. "Mnemba, you lazy *msichana*. Your guests have arrived. Get out at once and get your clothes on. I'll do your hair."

I scrambled out of the bronze tub as she handed me a fresh green towel, feeling resentful that I'd hauled buckets of water all the way from the river for such a short soak. The air was so heavy with humidity that the drops of water seemed to stick to my skin as soon as I climbed out. I hastily dried my body and hair, while Bi Trembla fetched a clean linen shirt and pair of trousers from the lone chest at the foot of my mattress. She shoved the items into my hands and began to roughly comb my hair back as I hopped into the trousers.

Her nimble fingers twisted my dark hair into tight cornrows. I pulled the shirt over my head, interrupting her progress with my stubborn hair. She huffed and yanked the narrow braids even tighter, while I stuffed my feet into my safari boots. When she was finished, she pushed me back to take a look at my appearance and sighed. "You're a pretty girl. I wish you would stop this nonsense in the savanna."

"I love what I do, Bi Trembla." True, sometimes, but even on days I hated it, working here provided my escape. Stumbling over my untied laces, I made for the door. Bi Trembla seemed ready to launch into full-out lecture mode, and I didn't want to get caught under her barrage.

"You won't find love here!" she shouted after me as I ran out of the hut, waving back at her.

Tumelo waited for me in the center of the main camp, holding a wooden tray with two glasses full of cold apple cider. He pushed the tray into my hands. "They are in my office, waiting for you. I offered to show them to their accommodation, but they want to ride out today, before it gets dark."

I already had a picture of the naturalist and his daughter in my mind. I imagined him as an academic in spectacles—a small man, with graying hair, unmuscled yet skinny in the way that only foreigners were. Once we got on the trail, he'd swap between swatting insects and talking a mile a minute about his research, desperate to find the creatures he'd only known on paper. His daughter would be typical of the women who came with me on the safaris—fragile yet demanding, unused to the exercise or the hot sun, armed only with a child's dreamlike fantasies of exotic lands and a blank sketchbook.

As soon as I entered Tumelo's hut, I realized the Harvings were like no tourists I'd ever guided before. Though their backs were facing me, I could see maps and charts spread out across Tumelo's desk. Mr. Harving's shoulders were broad, athletic, with muscles that showed through his practical, blue linen top. His daughter wore her long bright red hair tied back in a hasty ponytail, frizzy wisps standing up in the humid air. She too wore practical blue linen, light trousers and heavy black boots that I could see beneath the chair.

Usually, my efforts to make female tourists change clothes were met with a pitying sweep of the lady's gaze over my own attire. None of the female tourists from Echalend had ever worn trousers before. It might have been pity, not generosity, that had driven Mrs. Dyer to buy a dress for me.

"Good afternoon," I said, bringing the tray around to the other side of the desk and balancing it precariously on the only map-free corner.

Both Harvings got to their feet and extended their hands. Looking at him face on, Mr. Harving was older than he appeared from behind. His eyes were edged with deep wrinkles, but he had a smile so broad it almost ate up his face. A dark shadow of untrimmed whiskers framed his jaw.

Miss Harving looked about my own age. Definitely younger than twenty, with fresh, blemish-free skin. She had a fuller-than-fashionable figure, with soft, doughy curves rather than the waifish slenderness I'd come to expect from ladies in Echalend. Her eyes were impossibly ice blue, and they looked into mine with an intensity and excitement in them that made me suddenly want to study my shoes.

She took my hand before her father and wrung it with a man's grip. "Hello! You must be Mnemba? We're so pleased to be here and to have you helping us with our research. I'm Kara."

Her father took my hand next, pumping it eagerly. He echoed her sentiments. "Our ship was a cramped, rusty little bucket… hit all the storms, latrines a mess…. We could not be more thrilled to finally be here. This trip is the culmination of years of work for us."

Kara laughed, slapping her father's shoulder. "You only hated the ship because the captain kept threatening to throw you overboard." She looked to me with a conspiratorial wink. "It was fine. Our cabin was a bit small, but the crew were lovely."

"It's not my fault the man couldn't lose at poker," Mr. Harving mumbled.

Kara cleared her throat and exchanged a smile with her father. "Anyway, we are so pleased to be here. The trek will all be worth it for our research."

The way they talked about their research made it sound like something they did together, when I'd assumed it was Mr. Harving's occupation and she was just along for the trip.

I gestured to the tray. "Welcome to Nazwimbe. I have cold cider here for you. Tumelo—Mr. Nzeogwu—said you might want to go out this afternoon already? Are you sure you wouldn't rather settle in, have a rest, a bath? We can visit the—I'm sure Tumelo would love to show you some of our native games? The rides can be intense, especially after such a journey."

I prayed they might change their mind. I was scrubbed, reasonably sweat-free, and the sugar-buzz from the chocolate had started to wear off. Let Tumelo entertain them for a while. All I wanted was to climb into my bed and sleep the afternoon away.

"No, no. We've been traveling for *weeks* and spent months preparing for this before we left," said Mr. Harving. He gestured toward the maps. "We've been studying your geography. We have theories relating to the terrain and the breeding habits of the Kardunn. I can't wait to get out in the field and find some."

"The what?" I'd been a guide for Tumelo for over a year, and in that time, never heard of an animal called a "kardunn" before.

"Unicornalis Kardunn," Kara explained. She picked up a sketch of two animals. The drawing lacked the practiced refinery I'd seen in many of the ladies' sketchbooks, but I could make out the equine form of a unicorn and a smaller, two-horned beast that I couldn't distinguish. "That's their official name. We have this theory that the abada might also be a subspecies of unicorn, so we've classified them as a family."

My brain skipped over most of what she said, focusing in on a single word: unicorns. I almost sighed out loud. Of course Tumelo would assign me to this group, knowing that the unicorns were one of the hardest animals to track in Nazwimbe. What a bastard. The creatures lived a solitary existence, deep in the wooded brush, with prints indistinguishable from those of a common horse. They made no noise, moving with a feline grace, their whinnies a whisper on the air.

"How many days are you here with us in Nazwimbe?" I asked, moving Tumelo's box of cigars from his chair so I could sit in it. "Unicorns are difficult to track. We may have to go out several days just to see one."

"Mr. Nzeogwu assured us this area hosted one of the largest populations," Kara said, looking at me out of the corner of her eye with obvious suspicion.

"We're here for three weeks. Plenty of time! We understand they are elusive, part of their mystique that makes them so intriguing to us," Mr. Harving cut in quickly, taking a long drink from his glass of cider.

Great. Tumelo had all but guaranteed them I would find unicorns for them to study, even though he knew how difficult they were to find. He had been too happy to offer me four days off. I should have suspected something. Curses in two languages flashed through my mind. I'd known him for years. I should have realized that his generosity wouldn't come cheap.

"When can we be ready to go out?" Kara asked, wringing her pale hands. She began to repack the maps into long wooden tubes.

"I'll go prepare the horses," I said, taking a deep breath. I was so tired that heaving myself out of the chair seemed like an adventure in itself.

As Kara packed up the documents, one of the long carrier boxes knocked into the tray, spilling cold cider into my lap. I leapt to my feet with a yelp, the liquid soaking my trousers to the skin.

"I'm so sorry!" Kara was at my side in seconds, trying to mop up the mess with a white sweat towel, but only succeeding in pushing the stain deeper into the fabric. Her cheeks went pink with embarrassment, and she bit her lip.

I sighed; those were my last clean pair.

I moved away from her, trying not to grimace at the feeling of the wet fabric against my thighs. Schooling my face into a reluctant smile, I said, "It's fine. I'll change. Meet me at the stable block."

Chapter Two

IN TWO hours of scouring the red earth for tracks, I'd managed to locate a lone, undersized bull elephant. I searched the riverbanks for hogfish and crocodiles, the tree lines for leopards and *mngwas* and prodded the bushes as we rode along with the end of my rifle, hoping to draw out the *malaxas* and jackals. For once, even the phoenixes stayed hidden. As we turned back to take the path home, I felt sticky with defeat, sweat, and tree sap.

The Harvings praised the beauty and diversity of the flowers, the tremendousness of our vast, open spaces. Both were good riders, and rather than ignore me and chat to each other, they actively scanned the horizon with their binoculars. Their cheerfulness annoyed me. I almost wished they had spent the afternoon whining or trying to throw things at the elephant while it cooled itself in the mud, grasping leaves from above with its dexterous trunk. Then I could have resented them, instead of my own failure.

We rounded a corner in the path, passing alongside the riverbank. The water was high from the spring rains, brown with silt. A twitch in the bushes across the water drew my attention, and I squinted toward it.

"Look, look!" Kara said, standing in her stirrups and pointing. "A crocodile, there's a crocodile on the bank!"

I followed the line of her finger to a moss-covered log, bobbing in the current along the shore. I snorted. "That's a log, Miss Harving."

Kara flushed, twisting the dials on her binoculars. "No... it's moving...."

I reached over and plucked the instrument from her grasp, adjusting it myself. When I passed the binoculars back to her, and she peered through the focused lens, her blush deepened. If it was possible, the redness of her cheeks made her eyes even brighter.

"I just got these," she muttered.

Suddenly, Mr. Harving's horse let out a squeal and bolted. Tail held high, the horse put its head down and ran, long strides eating up the ground. My mare reared on her hind legs and fought to free her head from my iron grip. Even Kara's mount, a swaybacked, elderly gelding, pawed at the ground and grunted nervously.

As soon as Elikia's feet were on the path again, I saw what had set them off. An enormous griffin paced toward us, beak snapping open and shut. The animal's yellow, catlike eyes had narrowed into slits. Sunlight glinted off her silver feathers, making her appear covered by chain mail. Her tail twitched and her hind legs bunched beneath her body as she stalked us.

I looked to Kara, expecting her to be shaking with terror or crying. In my time as a guide, I'd seen my share of sobbing tourists. Instead, her rifle was cocked, and she stared at the creature down the barrel.

"Hold, don't shoot it. Not yet," I said, looking the griffin in the eye. One of the first things I'd been taught by Tumelo when I started guiding tours was that prey run. Alpha predators always stood their ground. To a griffin or a lion, humans who ran were no different than the impala and buffalo they hunted. Standing to fight could earn the hunters' respect.

The griffin made a warbling sound deep in her throat, like a disgruntled farm goose. She looked away from us, gazing into the brush behind her. The bushes rattled, and a flurry of tiny griffin babies swamped their mother's legs, winding in and out of her feathers and playing with the tuft at the end of her catlike tail.

Kara chuckled and put her gun up. We started laughing, and I felt the tension in my body gradually flood out. The griffin fluffed her gray feathers and lay down, the babies burrowing into her and tucking themselves under her protective belly. Tiny beaks and feathered heads popped out from under her bosom, peering up at us. Two of the bolder infants wobbled toward us, imitating their mother by clacking their beaks. The mother stretched out her paw and tucked the wanderers back underneath her.

"Aww, look at them! They're kind of cute," Kara said, patting her horse's neck. "In a monstrous kind of way."

"Where did you learn to use a gun?" I asked. When she'd requested a gun at the camp, I'd been shocked. And kind of suspected she'd asked just for show. Instead, her unwavering grip had demonstrated experience. The barrel had made a perfect line to the space between the griffin's eyes.

She shrugged and brushed her sweaty hair back out of her face. "My father thought I should practice before we came here. I set my old dolls and stuffed toys up in the hedgerows and practiced shooting them."

I imagined a row of smiling child's toys with bullet holes between their eyes. The morbidness of it made me chuckle.

Shaking the image out of my mind, I looked down the path. There was no sign of Mr. Harving or his horse. "We should probably look for him. I don't see him down the track. His horse didn't look like it would stop anytime soon. I'll find him a different mount tomorrow."

Kara laughed. "I'm sure he's fine. He's a great rider. Probably enjoying the chance to have a good gallop after so many weeks in wagons and on ships."

Although I'd ridden her a few times myself, Mr. Harving's horse was pretty new. She probably had never seen a griffin before, definitely not one poised for hunting. I would have to tell Tumelo about her behavior. The mare's inclination to bolt made her unsuitable for us. Our horses had to spook in place, as running only made them more likely to get attacked.

Lucky for me, the horse left deep, muddy hoofprints in the red path. We followed them at a trot until we found the horse grazing beside the path in a field, with no sign of her rider.

Kara sucked in a breath beside me. "He's lost. God, I can't believe this. Lost on our first day. Do you think something attacked him?"

I didn't want to say that it depended on how badly he'd fallen. Some of the animals in Nazwimbe could literally smell blood for miles. Falling off your horse with those things nearby never ended well.

"I'm sure he's all right, Miss Harving. He's probably back along the path somewhere, in a hedge or something. I was focusing on the trail and probably didn't spot him."

I steered alongside Mr. Harving's mare to grab her reins. Kara kicked her gelding back and forth down a small stretch of the path, calling her father's name, getting louder each time she yelled. I glanced about the field itself. Long blue grass whistled in the light breeze, the stalks swaying. The mare had trampled a flat square in the middle of the field, but I couldn't see a rider's impression. A blue mush of grass dripped from her bit. I scanned the edges of the field, looking around the tree roots for any sign of Mr. Harving.

"He's here, he's over here! Mnemba, quick!" Kara shouted from the edge of the forest, twenty meters farther back up the track. "He's not moving."

She dismounted, wrapping her horse's reins around her fist, then knelt down in the tall foliage. I could make out a tuft of her flaming hair shining like a beacon as I cantered toward her, dragging her father's reluctant horse behind me.

I swung off Elikia and crouched beside her. Kara had peeled her father's trouser leg up, revealing his swollen calf. A boil had formed along the man's curved muscle, red and swelling with a white center. I swallowed hard. "Help me flip him over. I need to see the other side of the injury."

"What if it's broken? Won't we risk moving the bone?" She laid her hand protectively across her father's chest.

"It's not broken. I think it's a sting, but I need to see it more clearly."

"A sting? A sting from what?" Her voice rose. "Is it poisonous? Oh no…."

Without thinking, I laid my hand over hers and squeezed it. Immediately, I tried to justify my alarming overfamiliarity with a client to myself. It was a maternal gesture, right? Comforting? Out here, she and her father were my responsibilities. My safari-children. Her hand was as soft as the inside of a flower petal and the milky color of unicorn ivory.

If she thought I had overstepped a boundary, she didn't show it. Maybe friends did that kind of thing in Echalend. Kara squeezed my hand back without looking at me. "If you're sure."

We turned him on his stomach, and I inspected the back of his calf. In the middle of the boil's white center was a black stinger, the length and width of my middle finger. I closed my eyes, worst suspicion confirmed. I slid my fingers to the man's neck as subtly as I could. I didn't want Kara to see me checking if her father was dead. His pulse beat strongly, and I relaxed. Bracing his leg with one hand, I pulled the barbed stinger out with the other. Chunks of white pus dripped from the stinger like goat's cheese.

I stood up and went to my saddlebags. Feeling around the bag's crumb-filled bottom, I found the small knife I always carried. I sat back down next to Mr. Harving. "You might want to look away for this. It's pretty gross."

Kara shook her head, her hair coming free from its tie and falling around her shoulders. I hadn't noticed how thick it was back in the office. She rubbed her father's back and watched my every move.

I slid the blade into the boil, making an incision the length of my thumbnail. A trail of yellow-green poison spurted out, the smell strong enough to make Kara gag. I braced myself and then squeezed the remainder of the toxin out through the opening. Pus and blood spilled down his leg in a waterfall of red and yellow. I imagined Bi Trembla's face, watching me conduct this field surgery without alcohol to clean the wound or a needle to seal it. Her mouth would be gaping with partially formed curses, her hands balled into fists at her hips. But if we left it, the poison would spread throughout his body. Even Bi Trembla would have to concede to that.

We waited, hardly breathing ourselves, while his shallow breath became deeper and more regular, and he slipped into a more peaceful sleep. The sleep didn't worry me. If a person survived a manticore sting, sleeping after the stinger was removed helped them recover. Still, Mr. Harving could be ill for up to a week. Manticore stings were known to cause fever, chills, vomiting, and sometimes hallucinations. The sooner we got him back to camp, and into Bi Trembla's regimented care, the better.

Elikia wouldn't run if we met anything else on the trail, so I decided to load him onto her and ride his mare back. I brought the reluctant horse right over to Mr. Harving and gestured to Kara. "I'll need your help to load him. I can't lift him alone. He won't wake until tomorrow at the earliest, and we need to get him back to camp."

If she had been any of my other tourists, I might have ridden back at hell speed to bring Tumelo. Somehow I couldn't imagine a Mrs. Dyer-type lifting her husband onto a horse, emergency or not. But Kara was different—I'd just seen her stare down a griffin, and she hadn't fainted at the sight or smell of her father's injury. When I told her what had to be done, her mouth set in a firm line and she nodded. Together we bent down and lifted her father's snoring deadweight off the ground.

THE *MKUU* scattered ash in a circle around Mr. Harving's sickbed. Tumelo had insisted on calling a local spiritual leader, to give our guests an "authentic cultural experience" even though neither of us practiced the ancient beliefs. Nor did anyone I knew. Bi Trembla rolled her eyes as she changed the dirty dressing on Mr. Harving's injured leg. But Kara watched the Mkuu with fascination as he placed a phoenix feather under her father's pillow and traced a square in putrid amarok musk between his eyes.

When the healer completed his ritual, Bi Trembla pointed toward the door. "My patient needs his rest and some *real* medical attention. Why must you bring in these wretched displays, Tumelo?"

Tumelo shrugged, grinning at her. "Maybe I think they work."

Bi Trembla's eyebrows rose so high they almost touched her hairline.

"Or maybe I just like a good performance every now again. And these guys are cheaper than bringing in actors."

I covered my mouth so Bi Trembla wouldn't see my smile. Her scowl grew more pronounced, and she shooed all of us out, shutting the flap behind us.

Since Bi Trembla had taken over the hut assigned to the Harvings as a hospital, we'd had to set Kara up in another. Luckily, with the Harvings as our only current guests, we had more available. But none were as luxurious as the one her father had paid for. So we tried to make the new one as comfortable as possible, lining the floors with our best rugs and buying new furs from the village at exorbitant prices. The local tanners smelled desperation and charged Tumelo double. Still, we had a standard to maintain. We couldn't let her travel back to Echalend and tell her circle of friends our hospitality was lacking or that the hut where she'd stayed wasn't like the one promised to her father. There were too many up and coming safari camps in Nazwimbe. If our reputation wasn't perfect, Tumelo's business would fail.

Kara followed us out of the hut, smiling for the first time since we'd returned to camp two days before. Her father's color had returned, and he'd taken a little clear broth. The two of us would go back out into the wild today.

I went to get the horses ready, sending Kara to the kitchens for a morning cup of tea and some hot porridge. Tumelo jogged up behind me, gasping for breath.

"I have a plan," he panted, bracing his hands on his knees.

I sighed. Things never went well when Tumelo had a plan.

"In case you can't find a unicorn. Since it's only his daughter going out with you for the next week, I can put a horn on Ketz and leave her in a field for you to find. That way if you don't find one when Mr. Harving is better, his daughter will still say she saw one. Then they can't go home and say I'm a liar."

I groaned. Ketz was an elderly gray mare, arthritic and boney with knobby knees and growths on her ankles. Unicorns had rounded, strong bodies. Kara would never believe she was a unicorn no matter how well Tumelo decorated the horn. "That's not going to work, Tumelo. She's not stupid. She helps her father with his research. And Ketz looks nothing like a unicorn."

"She's white-ish," Tumelo defended.

"And that's where the similarities end."

"Eh, Mnemba. They're foreigners. They've never seen a real one. They just know they look like horses, yeah?" Tumelo ran a hand through his hair, and a faint blush rose to his cheeks.

We entered the barn. Ketz was not tied to her post.

My eyes narrowed. "You've done it already, haven't you? Where did you leave her?"

"I used a real unicorn horn!" Tumelo protested. "I gave it to the kitchen boy to tie on. That girl will never know the difference! And I didn't leave the horse. The boy is out watching to make sure she doesn't get eaten."

"And who is going to make sure the boy doesn't get eaten?"

"I gave him a gun. Bi Trembla said he's reliable."

"You gave a ten-year-old child a rifle?"

"He's just small. I think he's twelve or thirteen."

I shook my head, sighing. For all his wily business sense and salesmanship, sometimes the stupid things Tumelo did made my head hurt.

"Where did you even find a unicorn horn?" I asked as I threw a saddle over the back of the black gelding I'd chosen for Kara to ride. When he puffed out his stomach to stop me tightening his girth, I slapped his belly. Unicorns almost never lost their horns. The spirals were even denser than the tusks of an elephant, and unicorns were peaceful creatures that did not use the horns to fight each other.

Tumelo shrugged. "Oswe found a pile of them. Out by the Olafrango Lake, all clustered under one tree. We took a few back with us. We'll see if we can sell them at the market. I know some people make jewelry out of them. They're in great condition. All the silver spirals still on. Maybe you should go out to the lake? With all those horns near, maybe it's a breeding ground and you'll find some to show her."

I frowned. A pile of horns all in one place? It sounded to me like someone else had gathered them with the idea to sell before Tumelo, but why leave their stock out in the open? I needed to see for myself. Even if we didn't find a live unicorn there, Kara could bring a horn back to study. I bit my lip to hide a smile, imagining how excited she would be to have a real unicorn horn to bring home as a souvenir.

I decided to saddle Tumelo's horse for myself, figuring that if I took Brekna, he wouldn't go sneaking around trying to put any more horses with horns out in the savanna for us to find. Showy and dramatic, like his owner, Brekna had a powerful gait, a long ground-eating stride and always went with a beautifully arched neck. I loved riding him but barely got the chance. Tumelo wouldn't ride anything else.

"Don't take Brekna," Tumelo whined, chasing after me out of the stable block after I'd tacked up both horses. "What if I want to go into town?"

"Sorry," I said, batting my eyelashes at him sweetly. "I've been leading so many groups recently that my mare's exhausted."

Kara stood in the camp's muddy courtyard, sipping tea from a cracked pottery cup. Her hair was loose, framing her face. Over the past few days, she'd developed a bridge of freckles across her nose and cheeks, choosing to forgo the sun hats most of the ladies wore while in Nazwimbe. Some of the skin on her burned chest had started to peel off in a way that should have been disgusting, but instead drew my eye down toward her bosom. I bit the inside of my cheek. What was wrong with me? When she spotted me leading the gelding toward her, she smiled widely, a dimple forming on her left cheek.

I wanted to believe the smile was all for me.

That pleasant delusion was short-lived. After setting her cup aside on a nearby stone, Kara approached and took the reins from me. She scratched the horse between the eyes and cooed. "What a beautiful boy. Look at those long legs. I bet you're fast, aren't you?"

I scowled and busied myself checking Brekna's girth again. Jealous of a horse. How pathetic was I? It had to be loneliness bringing on these feelings. This place was too isolated. There was no one else my age at the camp, and I had not gone home in over a year. I wanted a friend, someone to talk to—that was all. Not that being attracted to another female was unheard of in Nazwimbe. If both women were married to the same man, it was often actively encouraged. But I didn't think I was like that. I liked men, or at least I used to. It had been so long since I saw someone my age that I'd started to forget what it was like to have a crush on anyone, male or female.

Not that this was a crush.

When Kara started to adjust her stirrups, I cleared my throat and my thoughts. "Tumelo says we should ride for the Olafrango Lake. It's not far from here, but one of our other guides found some unicorn horns. Might be a good place to start looking."

Kara's gorgeous smile vanished. "Horns? Do the unicorns shed their horns like deer? We never thought they did…."

"No, they don't."

She nodded, brows drawing together with concern. "I see."

The last thing I wanted to do was upset her. "We'll ride there. Check it out. See what's been happening, okay? I told Tumelo I thought it was pretty strange already."

This time, when her cheeks dimpled and her smile returned, I knew it had nothing to do with the horse.

GETTING AROUND the Olafrango Lake proved more difficult than usual. With all the rain we'd had in the past weeks, the lake swelled over its banks and mosquitoes clustered in the air, as thick as fog. Our horses sunk up to their knees in the mud, floundering and grunting. Brekna squealed and tossed his head, lifting his legs as high as his chest in displeasure. I started to regret taking him just to annoy Tumelo.

Kara swatted a handful of mosquitoes away from her face. "Are we almost there?"

I nodded. As we left, Tumelo had told me to look beneath the ancient baobab tree. The tree was on the lake's left bank, its old weathered trunk split into three sections. I looked over at Kara and winced for her. Red bites covered her arms and forehead. For whatever reason, the bugs always seemed to love foreign blood. Maybe it tasted different and gave them some variety. I kicked Brekna forward into a stumbling trot. The sooner we got through the cloud of insects, the better.

As we drew closer to the tree, I could see that, as usual, Tumelo had understated the situation. Horns lay strewn around the tree's roots, some sticking out of the earth like an ivory forest. Others lay scattered in broken, glass-like shards. My mind whirled with questions. How had anyone found so many unicorns? Why cut off the horns, just to leave them here, like this? If Tumelo had taken the time to gather them, they had to have some monetary value. Otherwise, he wouldn't have bothered. Beside me, Kara gasped.

I dismounted to inspect the horns more closely. None of them were covered in blood splatters or fragments of fur. Instead, their flat bases appeared to have been carefully sawed off. I glanced around for bullets but couldn't find any metal casings. Whoever had done this had used live unicorns. And if they hadn't taken the horns, it was the creatures themselves they had wanted.

Kara dropped to the ground beside me, covering her mouth. "Is this a graveyard? Like elephants have?"

"No," I said. I showed her the smooth edge of the horn. "Look, it's been cut really carefully. Whoever did this took them alive."

Kara took the horn in her hands, turning it over with sad reverence. Suddenly, I hated myself for bringing her here. What was I thinking? She was a naturalist. She cared about these creatures. How could I have thought that an animal-loving researcher would want an ivory souvenir to show off at home? It was different for me. I liked the animals, but my real pleasure came from the safari itself—the hunt. I loved the exhilaration of tracking something wild through the savanna and coming face to face with monsters. That, and the open air of the plains, fresh and miles and miles away from home and everything that had happened there.

"I'm glad my father wasn't here to see this."

"I didn't know it would be this bad," I said, wishing now I had just gone along with Tumelo's stupid plot to disguise our horse.

"We have to find out what's happening to them." Kara picked up another one of the horns. This one was smaller, and with only two silver grooves winding around the base. Like a horse's teeth, the grooves indicated age. The animal was—or had been—only two years old. For a unicorn, that was still a baby. "You said unicorns are rare and hard to find. And from our research, we've guessed that they never gather in groups of more than two or three. There must be thirty horns here. How would someone even find that many unicorns?"

I didn't know how to answer her. As a guide, I'd spotted unicorns a few dozen times, but most of the time, I came across the same six individuals, who had made their territory around our camp. I distinguished them by the size of their horns, old scars, and demeanor. Perhaps Tumelo's lie to the Harvings was right after all. Maybe our area was some kind of undiscovered unicorn hotspot. Or whoever had done this to them knew some way to attract unicorns from miles away.

"It looks like they've just tossed the horns," I said, thinking aloud. "Nobody's arranged them like this or tried to steal them. Whatever they're doing, they're doing it right here, and it's not about the ivory."

"I'd understand if they were selling them." Kara held the horn close to her chest, like it connected her somehow to the creatures. "It seems as though someone went through a lot of trouble to make them look like horses. But horses are cheap here. We saw them in the market on our way."

There were records in our histories, stories that my father had told me when I was a little girl, of people who had tried to tame and ride the unicorns. The stories told how the peaceful creatures went mad in captivity, stomping and spearing their would-be riders to death. I picked up another one of the horns and examined its smooth edge again. There was no way the unicorns could pass as horses. Even with the majority of their horns removed, a stubby growth of bone would remain. Any buyer could spot the difference.

I shook my head. "Unicorns aren't tamable. Everybody in Nazwimbe knows that."

"So you think a foreigner did this?"

"Maybe, but they'd have to be here a long time to do all of this. And if any foreigners had passed through here, I'd probably know about them. There aren't a lot of towns to stop at out here."

A clap of thunder sounded overhead, and I looked up. The clouds were gathering into a dark blanket above us. When rain came to Nazwimbe, it arrived with the force of a vengeful minotaur. We needed to get inside and fast. I gestured toward the sky, and Kara looked up.

"We'd better return to camp before we get trapped out here," I said, checking Brekna's girth again. If the rain came and we had to run for it, the last thing I wanted was to slip around his belly into the mud. "Maybe your research notebooks will give us some ideas."

We mounted back up and picked our way back around the lake. Once we were on the other side of the water, I could just make out a white, equine-shaped creature on the horizon. My heart beat a little faster. If we found a unicorn now, maybe I could make up for what I'd just shown her. Apparently, Kara had seen it too because her free hand flew to her binoculars.

She put the binoculars down, eyebrows raised. "There's a horse standing over there with a horn tied to its head. With blue ribbon."

I smacked my forehead. Trust Tumelo to execute his plan with such arrogant sloppiness. A blue ribbon? Clearly he hadn't even checked up on what the new kitchen boy was doing. Idiot. We trotted over to Ketz, intent on rescuing her. The mare blinked placidly at us as we approached, her mouth full of grass. There was no sign of the boy Tumelo had sent to watch her. But the mare recognized Brekna and ambled forward to greet us.

"Who's idea was this?" Kara asked, bending in her saddle to untie the horn, giggling as she passed it and the ribbon onto me.

"Tumelo's. Of course." I rolled my eyes. "He's worried you'll go back to Echalend and tell everyone he's a liar unless I find some unicorns for you."

I took the horn, and Kara's fingers brushed my palm. Warmth traveled up my arm and settled in my stomach. When we turned for home, laughing so hard we barely noticed the drops of rain starting to fall, I started to think that maybe Tumelo wasn't such an idiot after all.

Chapter Three

NOTES, CHESTS, and maps divided the table like a mountain range of paper. Never in my life had I seen so many documents. Bi Trembla had been complaining that the Harvings had far too many things, enough to fill three huts. Ungrateful foreigners, she'd mumbled, expecting her to clean so many. Now I saw why they needed the extra room. Kara swam through the papers, scattering notes and fragments around Tumelo's office-hut, while I sipped peony tea and watched the chaos unfold.

"We've been working on this project for years," she said, licking her fingers to help separate the pages. "We have so many notes on the habits of these creatures... all from other people's anecdotes, of course... stories we've gathered from other travelers, interviews, sketches...."

"I'd help," I offered, resting my feet on the table and helping myself to a guava from Tumelo's bowl. "But I don't even know where to begin. Is there some kind of system to all this?"

Kara wrinkled her nose, and I couldn't help thinking how cute it was: small and poreless, perfectly situated between her bright eyes and rose-colored mouth....

I had to stop thinking that way. Rich, Echalender ladies came to Nazwimbe to find chimeras, unicorns, grootslangs.... If they took an interest in us at all, it was as one more curiosity to add to their list. A few of our guests had sketched my portrait, cataloging my face amongst the landscapes and grelboks. I was something else to tell their friends about at afternoon tea: *Oh, Mrs. Rebtree, you'll never guess... when I was in Nazwimbe, I befriended a native!*

"Not really," she said. She smiled as she located a particular document and set it to the side. "We've been trying to employ a secretary. But the last one we got only lasted three days before she and my father had an argument. Apparently she got rid of some papers because they were duplicates. He's paranoid we'll lose something, even if he knows we have copies."

"How did you get into all this?" I'd been wondering that since the start of their trip. From everything I knew about the culture in Echalend, I didn't imagine learning to shoot guns and ride astride were hobbies most wealthy ladies enjoyed.

Kara shrugged, shifting in her chair. "My mom died when I was very little. Creatures of all sorts have always intrigued my father, but the unicorns were what kept me interested. Some little girls love ponies; I fell in love with them. They're so majestic. He didn't know how to spend time with me. And he didn't want to leave me to the nannies to raise. So instead, we researched together."

It was nice that her father had cared enough to keep her that close. I wished mine had. I picked up one of the papers, biting my lip and squinting at the tight cursive script. While I could read Echalende, it took me a while to process. I took another sip of my tea, slowly reading the headline of one of the documents: *Unicornalis Kardunn in Foal.*

I pointed to the paper. "This one's wrong. It says here they're pregnant for eleven months like a horse. They aren't. I've watched some individuals go through it. They're not consistent. They have the baby when the weather's right or when the dam thinks it's a good time for the foal. Sometimes five months, sometimes fifteen."

She shook her head, scowling. "No, that can't be right. Animals don't have babies when they want to. It's a set amount of time for the young to develop inside them. Sometimes they can wait a week or something, but not so much variance. And five months? It wouldn't have time to develop everything."

Her words sounded so patronizing that for a moment I forgot to be polite. I was used to condescension from other clients who thought people in Nazwimbe were ignorant and backward, but from her, it stung. "It is right. I've seen it. I think I'd know better than these guesses."

I covered my mouth as soon as the words slipped out.

Kara looked down at the mass of papers around us. Her fingers tightened around the sheets she was holding. "I suppose you're right."

After a moment, she cleared her throat and asked stiffly, "How did you get into this? I didn't expect to see female safari guides. We know some people who have been to Nazwimbe before, and no one mentioned women leading groups."

"Tumelo is my cousin," I replied, knowing it wasn't much of an answer. My hand was covering my stomach like a shield. We both sat in silence, flicking through papers without looking at each other, until I finally broke. I never got to talk about what had happened. Even with Tumelo, I never mentioned it anymore. He'd given me a new home. A job. I didn't think he owed me anything else, and I was sick of the look of pity he gave me every time I brought it up. "I was attacked... and what he did... I'm not marriageable anymore. So I came here."

Kara lifted her head, searching my face for further explanation, and reached across the table to lay her hand on my wrist. Her fingers were freezing in the chilly morning air, but the gesture was so unexpected that I gripped her hand like a climbing rope.

She sighed. "I'm engaged. In Echalend, an astrologer pairs us at birth. Sometimes it works, sometimes not, but the king himself signs the documents, and we must agree…. Timothy is nice enough, I guess. But there's nothing between us. I don't think he wants me either. Not really. And he doesn't understand me. He thinks I'll grow out of all this, maybe take an interest in well-bred ponies instead. Because what's the difference, right?" She bit her lip and hid her pain in a downward sweep of her elegant lashes. "This is going to be my only adventure."

I didn't know how to comfort her, so I croaked out, "We'll make it a good one."

I looked back over the document in front of me. Kara didn't seem focused on our clasped hands, and I wondered if for her, I was filling in as a replacement for friends she missed, back in her own country. Again, I worried that this type of gesture was common in Echalend between friends. Still, that she could see me as a friend beat being one more item on a tour-of-Nazwimbe checklist.

Even though the Harvings' idea about the unicorn gestation period was wrong, something else in their notes struck me. Again and again, they mentioned the full moon or moonstones when they wrote about the breeding process. Apparently people from all over Nazwimbe had observed that unicorns gathered at the full moon or around moonstones to breed. Sometimes in pairs, other times in groups of up to twenty. Nobody could control the moon and its light graced all of Nazwimbe once a month, so it would be impossible for anyone to pinpoint a location.

But moonstones were small, easily portable. If someone created a collection of them, maybe they could draw a whole herd of unicorns together....

Grudgingly, I disentangled my hand so that I could push the document over to Kara. I pointed to the paragraph. "I think there is something to this. About the moonstones."

She smirked, eyes lighting up. "So, you're saying our research isn't entirely useless?"

I held up my hands in mock surrender. "I never said it was useless. Just that one little, itty bit of it might be wrong."

Kara scanned the document again, ignoring my comment. "So if they have these moonstones, they're probably putting them in the tree or near it, to draw the unicorns out?"

I nodded. Parts of this were starting to make sense, but we still had no idea why anyone would want to lure a herd of wild unicorns. Much less try to take them alive and leave their horns behind.

A slow grin spread over Kara's face. "We need a stakeout," she said. "Like they do in the military. Twenty-four-hour surveillance on the site."

I raised my eyebrows. None of my clients had ever requested to spend a night in the savanna before. Most of them thought sleeping in our huts was rough camping, never mind spending the night in a tent on the ground. I'd done it a handful of times with Tumelo, when Bi Trembla's snoring kept the entire camp awake. "Will your father let you do that?"

Kara shrugged, shuffling a few of the papers into a neat pile and folding them away in her pocket. "He's bedbound for another few days. We don't have to tell him, right?"

BI TREMBLA chased after me, her ostrich feather duster raised like a weapon. "You can't bring that white girl into the wilderness for the night! Are you crazy? She can't stay in a tent with the wild animals around! Does her father know?"

"Of course he knows," I lied, but Bi Trembla sniffed out my deception as keenly as a hydra smells fresh blood in the water.

She put her hands on her wide hips and smirked. "What if I tell him?"

"By the time you tell him, we'll be away. So you'll just make your patient all nervous," I said as we entered the stable block. "Do you want a nervous patient? Ringing his bell for you every five minutes, asking if his daughter has returned yet? Besides, Tumelo's okay with it."

"You think I care what Tumelo will allow? That boy is even less responsible than you are!"

"Well, technically he is in charge of this camp. Technically."

Bi Trembla scowled, frown lines thickening above her brow. We glared at each other, waiting to see who would back down first. "Fine," she said, jabbing her finger at my chest. "I will not tell him. But no harm better come to that girl. One night. And no sleep for you. You stay awake. And watch to make sure nothing tries to get into her tent. There are wild creatures out there... and wild men."

I waved her off, rolling my eyes. "Yeah, yeah. We'll be careful."

Tumelo had already packed the things we'd need overnight, as neither of us had planned to tell Bi Trembla at all. The woman had eyes all over the camp. Sometimes I suspected one of her parents was a troglodyte. I gathered the gear and began strapping the bags to the placid mules. As I finished, Kara tiptoed into the stable block, dressed from head to toe in black, as if trying to blend in to the dawn. She even wore a black-net covering over her hair.

I giggled. "You know camouflage won't help us escape, right? Bi Trembla is already on to us."

She put her hand to her mouth. "My father doesn't know, right? I thought if I wore black, he might not recognize me so easily when we ride off because he couldn't see my hair. His eyesight isn't what it used to be. He'll worry and I don't want him to be concerned when he's so sick." She pulled the net off her hair. "Stupid, right?"

"Bi Trembla's agreed to keep our secret for the time being. She doesn't want the extra work of caring for a nervous patient."

I finished saddling the horses, allocating her the black gelding again, as she seemed to enjoy a feistier ride. As I worked, I glanced over to the stall next to me to talk to her, and then hurriedly turned back to the horse, feeling heat rise to my face. Kara had stripped off her black shirt. Her face was hidden by the fresh tunic she tugged over her head, but her back was bare and her hair hung down, kissing the places beneath her shoulder blades.

I fished an apple I'd stolen from Tumelo's fruit basket out of my pocket, biting into its succulent sweetness. That way if she said something to me now, I'd have an excuse for mumbling back. Juice squirted down my chin and across my cheeks. Why couldn't I ever keep clean while eating?

From the next stall, Kara reached out and brushed it away with her fingertip, chuckling. Was she flirting? "You reminded me of my grandmother, so I had to wipe it away fast. She always drools when she eats."

"Thanks," I said, passing the gelding's reins to her and frowning. Couldn't be flirting if she was making comparisons like that. "I'm happy I remind you of your drooling grandmother."

She blushed and led her horse outside.

I tied the pack mules' leads to a ring on my saddle and mounted up. Kara climbed aboard and settled into the saddle with expert gentleness. I nudged Elikia, and we snuck out around the paddocks, careful not to ride past the hut where Kara's father slept.

The phoenixes always sang at dawn. As we rode along the path, their ephemeral voices rang out in harmony, almost like a greeting. Today we had a breeze and the humidity wasn't as stifling. For once, my skin felt dry. Kara closed her eyes to absorb the sound, smiling as the early morning sun bathed her face. She released the reins and let the gelding follow me. I noticed that Bi Trembla had given her a paste made of flour and baking soda to put on the bug bites to stop the itching. They looked less swollen today, and on her pale skin, the paste helped conceal the redness. After we pitched the tents, I'd search for some citronella roots to keep the bugs off her for good.

Instead of taking us straight to the cliffside where I'd planned to make camp, I led Kara through the woods to a little clearing along the river. Tumelo always thought we should feed each guest and ourselves for two, so the mules carted breakfast for four. Although I'd had the apple, my stomach rumbled. I was looking forward to digging out whatever my cousin had decided to pack. I held up my hand and pointed to the riverside, pulling Elikia to a halt.

We dismounted, hobbling the horses to let them graze. Kara took a seat on a rock by the river, dangling her fingers in the current and looking across the narrow body to the jagged cliffs that lined the other side. A waterfall slithered down between the rocks. I'd always loved this spot.

I pulled the packs off the nearest mule and searched through them. The first thing I found was a jar labeled "*Maziwa*—Kara, tea." I rolled my eyes. Tumelo had teased me about my appetite since I was a child and here he was, a decade later, still making sure I'd remember not to drink all the milk so Kara could have tea.

Before I had time to get all the breakfast things out of the pack, Kara had started unlacing her boots. She grinned wickedly at me over her shoulder as she pulled off her socks and tossed them onto the ground. "The water looks clean. You don't have leeches in Nazwimbe, do you?"

No, just *morgawrs*, hippos, and crocodiles…. The thought died as she unbuttoned her trousers. The stiff khaki slipped lightly to the ground. Her linen shirt fell to midthigh. Unwillingly, my gaze traveled down her legs, to the alabaster thighs with just a trace of dimpling above her knees.

"I need to check the area," I said too late, as she waded into the river.

"I'm all sweaty from the ride. I want to cool down before we eat," she called back, floating on her belly.

I scrambled to the shore. The river was clear and quiet. I couldn't see any trace of crocodiles basking in the sun. Sighing, I undid my boots and pulled off my own pants, following her knee-deep into the cold water, wondering how she could stand to swim when it was so cold. My teeth chattered and goose bumps prickled my arms. She edged her way over to the waterfall and leaned up against the cliff behind it, letting the water run down through her hair. White fabric melded to her ample curves like a second skin.

"Come on!" Kara said, leaning down to splash a fistful of water at me. "This is way better than the baths at the camp. I think the water is fresher here too. Farther upstream."

I stared at the pebbles rolling under my toes, too afraid to look back up. Warmth rose up my neck. Try as I might to focus on the brown and gray stones, I couldn't get the image of her form beneath the wet, clinging fabric out of my mind.

"Come out," I said, beckoning and chancing a glance up. "It's not really safe here to go in the water."

"I'm keeping my eyes peeled," she said and winked. Her teasing eyes looked into mine.

Something slippery brushed my ankle. I looked down but couldn't see the cause. A river fish, probably, or an eel. Maybe I'd try to catch a few for dinner later. A few feet away, something rippled in the water. From her position under the waterfall, Kara suddenly pointed. "Look, over there, a mermaid."

I whirled around. Sitting placidly halfway up the bank, a brunette mermaid sunned her hominoid half in the open air. She hummed a soft tune, something imitated from one of the birds.

Banishing all thoughts of Kara's magnificent body, I raced forward and grabbed her by the arm. I pointed to the nearest part of the shore. "Go, run! Now!"

She blinked at me in confusion, struggling as I pulled her toward the bank. "It's a mermaid. They're harmless. I know they can't actually converse like people, but they're still pretty to look at."

I'd heard people say that before. Foreigners and their ridiculous myths. Some of them believed mermaids were actually part human, with whole societies built under the oceans. Ocean mermaids were more solitary. Alone, no mermaid could submerge a human. But the river mermaids of Nazwimbe were amphibians that roamed in schools like fish. Where there was one, there would be more. A school of piranha had nothing on a group of mermaids. I'd seen them strip a water buffalo down to the skeleton in under a minute.

"Stop, Mnemba. You're hurting me," Kara protested, trying to yank her arm out of my grip. "It's all the way over there. You're being dramatic. Stop it."

"They're dangerous. We have to get out. There will be more around here somewhere." Strong as she was, fear helped me win. I tugged her up onto the riverbank.

"Look, I appreciate you're being a good guide and all, but the sailors up by us have seen mermaids as well. You think I don't know anything and that all the research we did is worthless, so you're trying to show me up. Do you think that I'm some vapid idiot from the North who can't defend herself? You can't just manhandle me out of the river with no explanation." Her hands went to her wet hips and she glared.

Annoyance and fear made me turn mean. "All you do is study things in books from a thousand miles away, so whatever you think you know—forget it. In Nazwimbe things you can't see can kill you. And sometimes we don't have the luxury of sitting around at a table batting questions back and forth."

"Thanks for reminding me that I'll never get a chance like this again. I already know that. Books from a thousand miles away are all I'm going to get," she snapped back, sitting down on the river's bank.

Angrily, I squelched, still sopping, across the grass to the mules and took my rifle down. A wild hare sniffed at the grass in the clearing. Without thinking further, I shot it. The shot was clean and the hare dropped. I stalked over, seized the dead animal, and tossed it into the river. Kara's face drained as its blood spread through the crystal water.

A tiny ripple appeared, and the hare's foot twitched as if nibbled by a small fish. Then, in a flurry of aquamarine tails, the mermaids pounced. Their slippery bodies twisted around each other as they snapped flesh from bone with razor sharp teeth. With a toss of her hair, the brunette from the banks dove into the blood-crazed fray.

Chapter Four

NEEDLESS TO say, we skipped breakfast on the riverbank. Kara dried herself and changed into a fresh shirt. She mounted without speaking to me. I couldn't decide if she was angrier I'd shot the hare to make a point or that I'd been right about the mermaids. Whatever her reasons, the silence hurt.

We rode on without speaking to each other—all the way to my planned campsite behind a ridge overlooking the Olafrango Lake and the fields below. From the higher vantage point, we'd be able to see everything that happened at the baobab tree without getting in the way of a frenzied unicorn orgy or risk being surprised by their hunters. I pitched the tents while Kara made a show of petting and speaking to the horses, ignoring me. She cooed over them, feeding them bits of grass and handfuls of dried fruit from one of the packs.

When I finished setting up the tents, I found a seat on a rock as far away from her as possible and took my binoculars out to study the fields below. We were here to find answers, not play with the horses. They probably would have been happier left to graze on their own anyway.

A herd of wildebeest browsed the grass below us in the open field, with zebra and abada dotted amongst them. Watching the two-horned abada peacefully munch grass alongside the other animals, I was suddenly curious what made Kara and her father think that they were another species of unicorn. True, they had an equine-style body, with horns and hairy legs, but zebra stripes wound up their hind legs and their tails were tufted like a great cat's. Their behavior was nothing like the unicorns: living in massive herds, grazing out in the open with little regard for humans or predators. Unicorns had a presence, a sense of majesty that the abada lacked. Since they wandered alongside the herds of wildebeest and zebra, I'd always assumed the abada was some sort of hybrid of the two.

I stole a glance over at Kara. She had stopped petting the horses and taken a seat herself, looking down the tunnel of her binoculars. Her head followed the herd, and I could guess what she focused on. A small foal trailed one of the abadas, head-butting his mother's side with his blunt baby horns. His gangly legs twisted, and he toppled forward onto his muzzle, whinnying until his mother nosed him back onto his feet. Kara's lips curved into a smile. I chuckled.

She looked up and scowled when she saw me watching her. Setting her mouth in a tight frown, she looked straight ahead again.

"Come on," I said, a little nervous now that she might not speak to me at all for the rest of the stakeout. And what would Tumelo do if she told him about my outburst? The camp couldn't afford to get a reputation for hiring rude guides with a temper. Maybe he'd finally do what my mama kept begging and send me home. "I had to drag you out. Those mermaids would have killed you. I'm sorry I shot the rabbit like that and didn't explain things to you, though."

Kara glared out across the field for a moment before sighing. She turned to face me. "I guess I'm not really angry with you."

I let out a slow breath in relief.

"I'm just angry that there is so much I don't know. There's so much that's not part of our literature at all. Most of our naturalists and scientists are away studying Zanchen and other places so far to the west. Nazwimbe is hard to get to. The only way is by ship and then by horse over land. The scientists that do come here, they all want to look at the griffins, hydras, leopards… killers." Her shoulders sagged. "I just wish I had more time to study and have a life."

I stood up and sat down on the rock beside her. "Can't you just turn him down? Or delay it? Is there a timeline?"

"I have two years. Since I'm younger than him, when I turn eighteen, we have to get married. It's the law."

"Some birthday present."

She laughed, but it was hollow.

I pointed out a group of baboons stooping by the edge of the lake to drink, hoping to distract her. She peered down at them, watching the babies dunk each other in the shallows. Slowly, she lost her thoughts in Nazwimbe.

The tourists who visited us always talked about how backward we were here, discussing the shortcomings of my country in front of me as if I were invisible. Our huts were too simple, our technology unrefined, our food too bland. We didn't have buggies, and the potholes in our dirt roads made them sick to their stomachs. No streetlamps replaced the stars as our midnight guides. Sometimes, when I listened to them talk about their libraries full of books, their jewelry, and big, multilevel houses, I envied all the things they had. But we didn't have a law that forced us to marry a person we didn't want. Men could take more than one bride in Nazwimbe, a practice Echalenders found barbaric, but only if all the girls were willing. They all had to want him. In Nazwimbe, our General horsewhipped those who forced a girl to marry outside her will, and bride prices were illegal. I valued that little bit of freedom more than oil lamps.

A cloud of dust appeared on the horizon, growing larger on the edge of the savanna. I picked up my binoculars again and focused in on it. I expected more wildebeest or maybe the water buffalo herd. They liked to come down for an afternoon soak in the lake's muddy banks. Instead I saw riders. A group of more than two dozen men cantered toward the ancient baobab tree.

Most of the men looked like highway robbers or beggars. They wore shirts strewn with reddish dirt and trousers so full of holes it was a mystery how they stayed on. Their bodies were lean, skin tough and ashy from days spent working in the sun. Pelvis bones and ribs jutted under their mounts' rain-rotted coats. But at the front of the vagabond cavalcade, an elegant businessman rode a foreign chestnut stallion. The stallion's coat was polished like a brass plate, and his body was fleshed with muscle. The man wore a top hat, black pants, and a red vest, the style many of the Echalenders favored, but his skin was dark.

"Kara!" I hissed. They were too far away to hear us, but the look of the gang made me nervous. We were not supposed to be here, I was sure of it. We were not supposed to see whatever it was they were about to do. If they saw us, who knew what they would do to make sure we couldn't give information away.

There were hundreds of baobab trees in Nazwimbe, but this one was especially remote with nothing but our camp for over fifteen miles. Their leader had picked it with care. The cliff sloped upward at the top, so our position concealed our stakeout camp, but while we sat up like this, gazing below, the men would easily see us once they drew closer.

Kara still sat angled toward the lake, watching the baboons chase each other and scoop algae out of the shallow water. She turned to me, her binoculars still held midair. I pointed toward the group. She looked down the lens and froze. We crouched low, looking over the ridge.

The men lined up, forming a crescent shape around the back of the huge tree. They dismounted, and one of them pulled a black box from his saddlebag. He scurried forward, bowing as he handed it to the man in the top hat. The leader opened the box and pulled out a semi-opaque stone the size of a watermelon. My jaw slackened. It was the biggest moonstone I'd ever seen.

He bent down and placed the stone in what looked like a hole in the ground. I twisted the dials on my binoculars, zooming in, and squinted. The hole was part of a long channel, narrow—a foot wide at most—that seemed to feed back into the lake. When we had investigated before, I'd been so transfixed by the sight of the horns that I hadn't noticed the canal. A definite failure for a tracker. The leader stepped back and accepted a flask from one of his followers.

The stone pulsed, then glowed white, casting an eerie light over the baobab tree. I felt the ground tremor.

For a moment, Kara and I sat with bated breath. I half expected a wild stampede of unicorns to materialize on the horizon beyond the lake. Instead we listened to the bored snorts of the horses below, the clash of horns as two abada stallions sparred off, and the ever-present, soft melody of the phoenixes.

Then Kara grabbed my arm. A charge of energy traveled from my wrist up to my heart as I turned to follow where she was looking. A lone stallion cantered across the field, whiter than summer clouds. His body heaved with muscle; thick feathers fanned his black hooves. Neck arched proudly, he carried a regal horn, twisted to the top with silver. The riders dismounted and reached for their lassos.

When he reached the baobab tree, the unicorn looked around in confusion. The trance of the moonstone seemed to break with the humans closing in on him. He sniffed the horns around him, squealing and pawing the ground in distress. Three of the riders threw their ropes, catching him around the neck. As he struggled to back away, the others advanced. Men taunted the stallion with their whips, making him kick and try to rear. When his feet lifted, they threw more ropes, circling the nooses around his powerful feet. As a group, they wrestled the unicorn to the ground, throwing themselves on top of him the moment his knees touched the grass.

Even with the weight of six on his back and men all around holding ropes anchoring him to the ground, the stallion kept fighting. His eyes rolled back in his head, his legs thrashed, and I could hear his screams from the cliff. I'd never heard a unicorn make a sound before, and hearing it now sent a chill through my entire body. His screams were different than a horse, higher in pitch, with a vibrating tremor that made him sound almost like a singer at the crescendo of a magnificent performance.

The leader of the group advanced on the now subdued unicorn, holding what looked like a handsaw. The stallion tried frantically to spear the man with his horn, but three of the followers held the animal's head in place. Still he tried, snorting and staring his captor in the eye, silver-tipped horn poised like a sword toward the leader's heart.

Kill him, I found myself praying. *Fight them. Kill him, and it'll all be over.*

The saw began to tremble in the man's hand as he swiped it again and again across the base of the stallion's horn. Fragments the size of fingernail clippings covered the earth like snow. Beside me, I felt Kara start to shake. Her whole frame quivered with silent sobs. The horn fell to the ground, and all at once the stallion quit struggling. The men climbed off him and loosened their hold on the ropes that bound him.

The group's leader reached for one of the ropes around the unicorn's neck. He turned and the stallion followed him, as meek as an old broodmare. His eyes seemed to blink back a heavy sadness, the only echo of his proud battle song.

THEY CAPTURED another before they rode away: a filly, small and with delicate-looking legs and bones. The men underestimated her, and I almost cheered when she drove her horn into the thigh of one of her would-be captors. When they finally wrestled her to the ground, her success cost her. The injured man's friends whipped her mercilessly until her white coat ran with dark blood.

When their dust trail cleared on the horizon, Kara pulled her knees up to her chest. Her eyes and cheeks were puffy with tears. She struggled to speak, but her voice choked and clogged. "I've never seen anything so awful. I've been dreaming about seeing the unicorns for years. When that stallion appeared, he was everything I'd ever imagined and more... beyond beautiful. And what they did to him... what they made him...."

I nodded, wrapping my arm around her shaking back.

"I want to know what they do with them," she said, wiping her eyes and peering up at me. "I have to know."

"I don't think we want to know."

She lifted her head from my shoulder and looked me in the eye. "No, I have to know. Not knowing is the worst for me. I'll imagine everything possible. We have to find out. Please."

The way her blue eyes widened would be my undoing.

I knew those men were dangerous. They carried guns and whips and braved the unicorn's sharp horn to get what they wanted. If they could wrestle down a 1300-pound unicorn stallion, a beast made of solid muscle, what could they do to us? Plus, I'd never seen a stone like that before. It seemed to harness energy from the lake. But, against all logic and sense of self-preservation, I found my mouth forming the words: "It's only noon now. We still have the night and the morning tomorrow before anyone will expect them back… if they've not gone more than a few miles, I could track them."

Kara sprang up. "Tell me how I can help."

"It's not safe," I warned, climbing slowly to my feet. My knees ached from crouching so low for so long. "Bi Trembla will hang me from my feet and skin me alive if she ever finds out I agreed to this."

I didn't say that Tumelo would fire me, even though I was sure he would. Cousins or not, there was only so far I could push. This would cross the line. I had avoided my village for so long that the camp had become my home. I closed my eyes to clear a wash of nostalgia. At least if he sent me home, I'd be out of reach of Bi Trembla's wrath.

"I won't say a word," she whispered. "My father can't know either. He's progressive, but he would keep me chained to his side until I marry if he learned I went chasing after a poaching gang."

I spat into my palm and offered it to her. When Kara wrinkled her nose in revulsion, I chuckled. "That's how we seal a deal in Nazwimbe."

She rolled her eyes but spat into her own hand and shook mine.

I dismantled the tents while Kara grouped the horses together, tightened their girths, and offered the mules some water from her canteen. It wasn't ideal, tracking a group while dragging three pack animals behind us, but there was no way we could bring them back to the camp without raising Bi Trembla's suspicion. When I went tracking for practice, deep out in the wild, I liked to go with just my horse, another person, a gun, and enough water to survive. I could find shelter beneath a tree, or sleep under the stars, gather berries, and hunt rabbits. Traveling light made it hard for someone—or something—else to follow your trail, while you followed them.

We mounted up and carefully steered our horses down the ridge to the base of the baobab tree. I could see the area where the two unicorns had fought for their freedom. A jagged circle of frantically trampled grass and the heavy impressions their knees made on the soft earth remained. Kara dismounted again and went to retrieve the stallion's horn. She ran her hands along the silver ridges and then tucked it into one of our supply packs.

"I can't see which one belonged to the filly," she said, putting her foot into her gelding's stirrup and swinging back on. "There are so many smaller ones. I almost feel like we should bury them. The horns, I mean. It's like the unicorns' spirits just died the minute those men cut off the horns."

"In Nazwimbe, we burn the dead. We could try to burn the stallion's horn when we make camp tonight. Wherever that may be."

A broad smile appeared on Kara's face, but her eyes remained downcast. "I'd like that. And I think it's right, to do it the Nazwimbe way. He was from your country, born and bred."

I'd never tried to burn ivory before. I didn't even know if it was flammable, but for her, I would try. I would build the biggest brushfire ever seen on the savanna if it made what she had just seen a little easier to deal with. I pointed to the line of trampled grass leading away from us. "At least those men won't be hard to track. I don't even have to dismount to look for hoofprints. That many riders will leave a clear trail leading right to them."

She nodded. "Easy."

I shrugged, hoping I wasn't overselling my abilities. "Unless they split up. Then we'll have to choose which trail to follow and pray we're right."

IN A sense we got lucky. The riders stayed together, but we kept riding into the early dusk with no sign of their destination. Our horses started to tire, and the mules refused to trot on, leaning their weight against the leads that tied them to Elikia's saddle. The mare pulled to a stop, looking over her shoulder at the live anchors dragging her back.

With the sun going down, we needed to find a place to stop and make a fire. Most of Nazwimbe's hunters prowled the open plains in the haze of dusk and cover of the night. The riders had moved through the plains, along flat ground. I didn't want to lose the trail, but I also wanted to avoid making our camp out in the open. As we rode under the cover of a lone baobab tree, I reached up and cut a branch down with my knife, sharpening it into a stake to drive into the trail.

I chose a spot for us atop an old cheetah's den, a rocky outcrop with a dugout burrow beneath, and built our fire at the center. I fed it brush and heather, making it smoke so it would frighten the animals around us out of the underbrush. A smoky fire would also keep the insects that loved Kara's blood at bay. Kara gave the horses water, took their tack off, and hobbled them so they couldn't run away while we slept. True to my promise to Bi Trembla, I didn't intend to sleep, but I didn't think Kara would go to bed if she knew I was staying awake all night to keep watch.

I started to pitch the tents, assembling the first one in minutes. Our travel tents were simple, triangular structures with only four pegs. But as I put the first peg of the second tent in the ground, Kara walked up behind me. "I don't want to stay alone after seeing those men. Just put up one tent. They're not so small. We can cuddle close," she said.

Her words almost made me choke. I paused, keeping my eyes fixed on the peg, afraid of what my face might show her. "Are you sure?"

"Yeah," she said, her fingers wrapped around mine to pull the peg out of the earth. "It'll be like when I was at boarding school. We can stay up late and tell each other stories. It might take our minds off what we saw today."

I couldn't help it. When she wrapped her fingers over mine, my whole body involuntarily shivered.

"You cold?" she asked. I couldn't tell if her question was serious or not. "I packed an extra shawl in my saddlebag."

"No," I managed to squeak back. A whole night, alone in a single-person tent with her. How could I spend the night swapping stories in the firelight, when I wanted nothing more than to run my fingers through the flames of her hair and press my lips to the skin of her back? Those thoughts terrified me. Where had they come from? Part of me longed to be with her, to explore her. But a deeper part of me feared what it would be like to make myself so vulnerable, to let someone touch me and look at my scars.

Despite the warmth of her hand around mine, I felt frozen. I kept still while we held the peg together without putting it down. What did she mean, holding my hand like that? I swallowed. This was her adventure. *I* was part of her one adventure. But when she didn't move to release my fingers, I let myself wonder, for just a second, if it were possible she wanted what I did and if she felt vulnerable too.

When I turned to face her, her grip on my hand tightened. Color had risen to her face. Her pale cheeks and freckled nose glowed a soft pink. Specks of firelight glistened in her eyes. Her lips were so full and wet....

I leaned in and pressed my mouth to hers. I felt awkward, unsure of what to do, or how she would react.

Once upon a time, a man kissed me on the mouth, and his tongue forced its way inside like a gag, drowning out my screams.

I closed my eyes against the pain of the memory, damming up the flood of tears. I tried to relish the softness of her mouth pressed closed against mine and the tiny step she took toward me, her free arm curving around the lower part of my back.

Her tongue teased my mouth open. Instead of forcing, demanding, it suggested and coaxed. When my lips yielded, her tongue was cool with the water from her canteen. This time, it didn't feel like an invasion, and I felt my body melt into her flesh.

She led me into the tent by the hand, and I lay down on my back, waiting. I still wasn't sure what was expected of me. Or that I was ready. When my mama had told me about what women must do, in marriage, she had told me to do my duty, to wait for the man's lead and let him take his pleasure. I could take my own if I could, but always, my job was to please him. What did you do if there wasn't a man to please? What did you do if experience had already taught you to expect only pain? How did Kara get the confidence to do this? It seemed so natural for her. A knot formed in my throat, and I wondered if it would ever feel natural for me.

Kara began to kiss my neck, easing the tension. Her fingers slipped beneath my shirt to pull it off. I surprised myself by letting her, trying to relax as her fingers mapped my body. But when her eyes fell to the deep white scars spanning my stomach from the top of my ribs to below my navel, I crossed my arms to hide the marks.

"I can't," I said. "We can't go further. Stop."

She looked me in the eye, waiting. I closed my eyes again. My heart beat so fast it shook my entire body. With slow precision, she kissed each of the scars and laid her head down on my stomach.

"Your tiger stripes," she breathed, tracing over the crooked lines with her finger. And in that moment of complete acceptance, I knew I would never be the same. "They show how you resisted. They're like your battle scars. Don't be ashamed of them."

My fingers threaded through her hair, relishing the lightness of it, the sweet fragrance trapped within the layers.

A tear ran down my cheek, and I was glad her head was turned so she couldn't see. All this was just temporary—her one adventure—and she could never be mine.

Chapter Five

DESPITE MY promise to myself and Bi Trembla, I dozed off. When I awoke, Kara's head was still resting on my stomach, and I could feel the warmth of her sleeping breath on my bare skin. Carefully I moved her head down to rest on the tent floor, arranging her thick hair like a cushion around her.

In Nazwimbe, the day's heat vanished with the sun, and the air outside was crisp and wet. Our fire still simmered. Scanning the grazing horses, I counted them and breathed a sigh of relief. At least I hadn't been asleep so long that our fire went out and a predator snuck up on them. I knelt to feed the fire fresh kindling and brush, poking it gingerly with the sole of my shoe to stir it up again.

The flat plains spanned around the cheetah's roost. Somewhere far in the east, a soft glow loomed on the horizon. The light didn't flicker the way a single campfire would, and it was larger, spanning an area, though I couldn't make out any buildings. As far as I knew, there were no towns in this part of the savanna. The plains were a dangerous place to build: exposed, bare, full of the predators that stalked in the night. When I'd started guiding for Tumelo, I had memorized the maps of the area. A year ago no towns or villages had existed out here.

When I'd marked our trail with the peg, we'd been heading east. My heart started to pound with fear. The light looked too bright to come from the campfires of even two dozen men. I had to be looking at a town, but where had it come from? And why had it been built?

The tent flap opened behind me, and Kara climbed out. She had a wool shawl wrapped around her otherwise naked body. She sat down next to me, the peach fuzz of her legs brushing against my arm as she began warming herself at the fire.

"It's so quiet out here," she said, drawing the shawl tighter about her shoulders. "I've never been somewhere so quiet. In Echalend, people are always rushing about, even at night. Dogs bark. You hear the horses outside on the cobblestones."

I nodded. It was quiet at the camp too, but not like this. The smoke of our fire drove away even the crickets. Out on the savanna, at night, it was almost like the world stopped.

Almost. I pointed to the east, and Kara's eyes followed the line of my arm. She looked at the light in confusion and asked, "Is that a town? I thought most people in Nazwimbe lived in the mountains."

"It wasn't here a year ago, when I learned all the routes and maps."

Her mouth set into a grim line. "It has to be where those men went."

"Could be. Let's hope. Because if they went through it and didn't stop there, finding their trail on the other side is going to be a whole lot harder."

"Maybe the town's people would know where they went. A group that large, someone would have to know."

I shrugged, not wanting to tell her that if the men really were a gang of poachers, no one would tell us about them even if they did know. Villagers feared men who carried guns, enough to keep secrets for them in exchange for the illusion of protection. Men who carried guns *and* captured wild unicorns would terrify them.

"You'll have to cover your face and hair," I said reaching out and giving one of her red curls a light tug. After last night, it suddenly felt easy to touch her. "Full sleeves. I have some gloves in the saddlebags. If they see your hair or your features, the whole village will talk about you. We need to blend in."

Kara raised her eyebrow. "How am I going to blend in? In this heat, with all these clothes on?"

"A lot of merchants from Sylbaia come dressed like that. It's their culture."

Kara nodded. Then she rose to her feet. She went to the saddlebags, taking out my gloves before fishing out the unicorn's horn as well. She sat down again, turning it over in the firelight. Then she pushed it into the flames.

The horn itself held its shape, blackening without burning. But as we peered deeper into the fire, the lines of silver twisting around it unfurled. Starting from the wide base, a strip of pure silver filament unwound in a curled spiral. The glistening metal started to glow orange and red with heat, and suddenly, it exploded. The pieces hovered in the air around us, like stars suspended in midair. We watched them twinkle for a moment, before a low wind came and brushed heaven's dust away.

THE CLANK of iron greeted the dawn with us. As the sun rose, and I prepared the mules to leave, we heard the sound of metal and the low groan of a hundred men working in the rising heat.

Kara wrapped her shawl around her hair like a headscarf, donning my gloves and jacket. Only her eyes were visible through a narrow slit in the fabric. But as long as no one saw too much of her tapered features, hair, or body, people would assume she was a foreign merchant or a leper. At least I optimistically hoped they would, since we had no better method of disguise.

"I'm going to sweat to death wearing this," Kara complained. She lifted the back of her blouse, using the material to fan her sweaty body.

"Once we get through to the other side of the village, you can take it off," I promised. "We'll have a quick look around. Our towns aren't big, and this one can't be huge. It's been here six months at the longest."

I boosted her up onto Elikia, letting her step up using my knee. My mare was tall and narrow, difficult to mount from the ground. But her wiry frame and bay coat were more typical of horses here than the glossy black of Kara's chunky gelding. Better to have one less thing to attract attention to her.

We rode across the fields. Flower petals and old leaves whipped around us on the morning breeze. I reveled in the cooler morning air, letting it kiss the bare skin of my arms, while Kara sweltered in silence. I'd warned her not to speak once we left the relative safety of our little camp. Nothing would draw attention faster than her strange language and accent. And who knew if the poachers would have scouts lurking.

As we drew nearer to the village, it became clear that it wasn't a town at all—but a giant camp. I could see that none of the structures were permanent. There were no huts or chieftains' builds, nor farm animals and crops. Instead, hundreds of tents stood clustered together on a flat plain of mud. Each tent had only a single post, and they looked flimsy, like thin blankets that had simply been draped over sticks. Meat bones, half-smoked cigars, and molding bread littered the ground. Skinny pack mules picked through the garbage for scant mouthfuls of grass and leaves. A few men smoked pipes outside their tents or played cards. A few lay immobile on tattered pallets. Their cheeks were drawn together and their eyes bloodshot. Most didn't even look up as we passed them. One of them sported fresh whip marks across his back and shoulders.

We followed the sound of hammer against steel. My pity for the men intensified as our horses floundered in the deep mud— how could they live like this? Sleeping, eating, going about their lives up to their knees in mud and filth. Whippings were often given in Nazwimbe for crimes, but with the condition of the camp as well as the men's bodies plus the vacant look in their eyes, it seemed more likely that all of them were slaves, kidnapped from their homes. I wondered where they had come from and who had taken them.

The hidden location of the camp made complete sense now. The savanna was so expansive that it concealed many illegal operations; it was too difficult for the General to patrol hundreds of miles of open wilderness. Smugglers, drug traders, and thieves worked out here. I'd never seen such a huge camp before, but General Zuberi was getting old. Maybe he simply could not keep such a close eye on our frontiers anymore.

A rider approached us at a canter. His thigh was bandaged, and I recognized him as the poacher the filly had impaled the day before.

He spread his arms out, taking in the sight of Kara. He looked at her but spoke to me in our own language. "Ah! This must be one of the dealers. I thought it would be a man. Tell her she can unwrap. The sun is not too warm yet. I know these foreigners don't like to burn, eh?" He winked.

I hesitated, my mind churning and trying to figure out how we could turn this to our advantage. "My client is the emissary," I began shakily. "The dealer wants her to make a report before he rides here."

The man shook his head and rolled his eyes. "Worse and worse. These lazy Echalenders. I told Mr. Arusei we did not need all this foreign money. Local labor can provide what we need."

I shrugged, then cleared my throat and spoke to Kara. "Miss, the man here says you do not need your wrappings. The sun is not too hot, and you will not burn. He will show us around, and we can make the report to the Echalender dealer."

I noticed the way the poacher tried to follow what I said and was glad I hadn't spoken to her without breaking character. Kara cocked her head in confusion, but a moment later, she nodded and began unwrapping her shawl. I wonder what kind of dealer we were supposed to be representing. Surely hornless unicorns wouldn't fetch enough foreign money to be worth the hassle and danger of trapping them. Not when the creatures couldn't survive in a colder climate anyway.

When Kara's hair tumbled over her shoulders, and she revealed her face, the man smirked. "What a treat on the eyes, eh? That hair! And nice and fat. I'd lay that girl on her stomach and spend the whole day grinding into her behind. Probably why they sent you with her instead of a man!" He laughed, revealing a cracked tooth. I wanted to break the rest. I was glad Kara couldn't understand what he said.

I frowned, looking out over the camp. "Show us around so that we can make our report. It's a long ride back."

The poacher scowled, unhappy to have his survey of Kara cut short. "Fine, fine. Come along."

We followed him through the camp, trying to stay on the narrow path of solid earth behind him. It kept the horses out of the deep mud, so I wouldn't have to oil their legs later. The tents were everywhere, an endless sea of green and black tarp.

The men's groaning and the clap of metal grew louder and louder. The forest of tents slowly thinned out, but stretched out in front of us were dozens of laborers, carrying hammers, sheets of metal, wooden planks. Mixed in amongst them, I saw the unmistakable forms of twenty unicorns, their bodies strikingly white against the muddy black of their legs. Each unicorn pulled a sleigh loaded with metal. The scraps were piled high, twelve feet or more, and must have weighed several tons. Still, each animal pulled its own sleigh, its muscles barely straining with a load five horses would have struggled to drag. Overseers marched behind them, whipping both the unicorns and the laborers.

At the epicenter of all the activity, laborers lined the wooden planks and scraps of metal together in neat rows. They nailed the wood into place, adding rows to the great river of metal that stretched back farther than I could see, cutting through the savanna.

"It's a railway," Kara breathed.

"It's good?" our guide asked, gesturing to the scene in front of us.

It was the worst thing I'd ever seen.

My hands shaking on my reins, I whispered back, "It's good."

WHEN WE arrived back at the safari camp, bedraggled, dust-covered, and hungry, it was almost evening again. At the sound of our horses' hooves, Tumelo and Bi Trembla came running from his office. He held Kara's bridle while she dismounted, making a show of escorting her back to her tent for tea and a hot bath, all the while glaring at me over his shoulder. I gulped. His look was foreboding enough, but if he was leaving me alone to face Bi Trembla's wrath, he had to be furious.

Bi Trembla slapped the back of my head and then pinched my ear between her yellow nails. "One night! You promised me one! And that you'd have her back early the next morning! We've been waiting all day. Do you know how many excuses I had to make to her father today? Oh, they are riding. Oh, they have gone to the lake. Your daughter? Ah, she is having her nap. Stupid, irresponsible girl!"

I yelped, jerking away from her brutal nails. "We found something and had to track it. It took a bit of extra time. But we're back before nightfall!"

I didn't want to tell Bi Trembla *what* we had been tracking. Better to save that information reveal for Tumelo, after he took his evening drink.

Bi Trembla placed both hands on her wide hips and glared. "Do you know how worried I have been? Thinking for the past ten hours that a wild beast ate you in your tents? A stampede ran you over? It's bad enough that Tumelo sends a young girl into the savanna with only a bunch of idiot foreigners for protection, but how much worse if you didn't come back?" She reached out, and I cringed, thinking she was about to slap me again. Instead, her warm palm caressed my cheek. "I care for you, msichana. Like my own granddaughter. Make sure you always come back."

Done with her brief display of emotion, she picked up the basket of washing she'd left by the side of Tumelo's hut and bustled away. Tumelo appeared from behind a tree. Apparently he'd been waiting until after Bi Trembla finished with me to make his reappearance.

"That was quite a stunt," he said, pulling a cigar from his back pocket. "Want to tell me where you've been?"

I sighed. There was no hiding what we'd been doing anymore. Not when we'd already decided that we needed his help. "You know the pile of unicorn horns you told me to show her?"

Tumelo scowled. He knew me well enough to know there would be much more when I started things like that. "Yes."

"Well, we found out why they are there."

He stroked the day-old stubble around his chin. "Don't be coy, Mnemba. Spit it out. What have you found and why are you back so late?"

"They're capturing the unicorns," I blurted. "Taking them to build some iron road. When they cut off the horns, the unicorns just change… they give up. It's like a part of their soul dies."

"Back up," Tumelo said, lighting the cigar and sucking in a breath. "Who is capturing the unicorns?"

"A gang of poachers. They've brought the unicorns to the edge of the savanna. We saw them capture two. They're building… and kidnapping laborers, hundreds of them." My voice trembled as I remembered what we had seen.

Suddenly, I didn't care if he was angry with me. I stepped up to him and rested my head on his broad chest. My head fit perfectly under his chin. Tricky, mercantile bastard that he was, Tumelo had always been the family member I trusted. When everyone else had pressured me to just forget and live my life as a shell, he offered me a new start. Even when I thought any chance of a real life had vanished. His strong arms wrapped around me, and I poured out my soul, telling him everything.

"Hey," he said, petting my hair gently when I finished. "What you saw out there. It's all right. It didn't come back with you."

I shook my head. "We have to go back."

Tumelo pushed me off his chest to look in my face. "Why would you go back there? They have guns; they're kidnapping people. We should stay as far away as possible and go to your father. He has the General's ear."

"I don't have enough facts yet. We don't have proof that they're kidnapping the people or that the General doesn't already know. Like I said, we only had a quick glance around.... My father won't listen to us unless we have actual facts and know why they're building that railway." My voice trailed off, and I cleared my throat. "We need you. You and Mr. Harving. To pose as dealers."

He spat out his cigar midpuff. "Have you lost your mind? We can't ask a *tourist* to infiltrate something like this. It's bad enough you dragged his daughter into this."

"These unicorns mean the world to him. And to his daughter. Their life is studying these creatures. Plus, I didn't 'drag' Kara into anything. She wanted to go after them. She begged me."

Tumelo thought for a long moment, studying me. I squirmed under his scrutiny. "I've been thinking this whole thing, this tracking the poachers... it's not like you. You're like me. We leave well enough alone, unless it affects us," he said. "Why go after the unicorns at all? Why camp to watch these poachers? It's not the creatures themselves, I know. It has to be something else. So tell me, cousin, what is this girl to you?"

"A friend." It was the truth and a lie at the same time. "And I do care about the unicorns. You didn't see what happened to that stallion."

Tumelo cupped my chin, a knowing twinkle deep in his brown eyes. "Be careful. I brought you away here to see you happy, not to let you get broken again."

Chapter Six

I FOUND Kara reclining in her bath, hair draped over the side of the bronze tub. She didn't look up when I pushed back the hut's flap. Her head lolled to the side, and she dozed on her arm, while the steam rose in smoky white tendrils around her. Her flesh was bright pink with the heat, like the feathers on a hoopoe's crest. Bi Trembla sat on a low stool in the corner and darned the holes in Tumelo's woolen socks.

She looked up when I came in, cooing, "Poor lamb. Fell asleep almost as soon as she got in the water." Her brows furrowed, and she scowled at me. It wasn't fair that I got all the blame, and Kara was the "poor lamb," when she'd been the instigator. "You exhausted her in the heat. They're not used to it like us. You have to take each day slowly. I've just been watching here to make sure she doesn't drown. Her father is anxious to see her. She didn't want to go in until she washed."

"Don't you have cooking to do?" I asked, ignoring her accusations the best I could. The sun had almost entirely disappeared. Sometimes Bi Trembla insisted on doing too many things herself, which did nothing to make her sweeter. "I can make sure she doesn't sink."

Bi Trembla peered out through the flap, sighing. "So many things to do. Yes, I should start the cooking. Tumelo will get moody without his supper, and we're getting some more guests tonight—a couple, and they're late. Oswe is waiting for them at the end of the road with a candle."

I pointed to Kara. Her head had rolled back onto the edge of the tub. "I can do this, Bi Trembla, honestly."

"Her hair hasn't been washed yet," Bi Trembla said, getting up from her seat and packing up her knitting bag. She picked up the stool and moved it to the edge of the tub. Kara didn't stir. "Make sure you scrub right down to her scalp to get it all clean. She has so much hair, the dirt gets trapped."

"I know how to wash hair."

"Don't take that tone with me, I still haven't forgiven you. We have a standard to maintain."

I nodded and took a seat on the stool. Bi Trembla wearily stumbled out through the flap without glancing back. Kara's long hair hung almost to the floor. Next to the bath, she had placed a narrow comb, a soft soap, and a bottle of fragrant oil. I lifted the oil to my nose and breathed in a blend of thistle and vanilla.

I wet my palms in the hot water to warm them. Then slid my fingers through the layers of her hair, massaging the base of her scalp. She gave an unladylike snort, stirring from her sleep. I saw the shadow of her eyelashes blink in the dim light.

Slowly, I increased the pressure of my fingers, massaging behind her ears and up to her temples. I'd washed many ladies' hair before, but this was different. My fingers seemed to buzz with energy. The scent of the oil and the warm steam seemed to caress me and draw me into her. Kara tilted her head back and sank deeper in the water. "That's amazing, Bi Trembla," she sighed.

I chuckled, and she turned around, her lips pressed together in a mocking scowl. "Sneaking up on a lady in her bath. Not very proper. Is that the kind of establishment you run here?"

I dipped my head in a bow. "But, Miss Harving, I'm here to attend you."

She rolled her eyes but faced front again, leaning into my touch as I worked the soap and oil into the red tresses. Wet, her hair looked a different color. Like faded bronze, instead of brilliant copper. My own hair was so dark, I never noticed the difference, even when it was wet.

When I finished washing her hair, I rested my hands on her shoulders. Kara turned to face me, water running down over her lips. She reached up and hooked her fingers into my hair, yanking me toward her with a little growl. I moved back so quickly I nearly fell off the stool, biting my lip and looking toward the flap of her tent.

"We've kissed before," she said, scowling.

Nervousness made me shiver. How could I explain to her that every time might feel like the first to me?

"I can't."

Sighing, she dropped her hands back into the tub. "Are you afraid that it's wrong?"

"No… it's just… don't pull on me."

When she didn't respond, I lowered my head and kissed the hollow juncture between her shoulder and neck. She shuddered as my lips brushed across her collarbones.

I closed my eyes to preserve the scent of her in my memory. In two more weeks, she would get back on a boat and vanish forever. I wanted to ask her what this meant to her. Would she remember my scent too when she left? Or would I dissolve into a single piece of her memory of Nazwimbe?

Kara purred like a chimera in the sun and turned to face me, waiting for me to lean toward her. On her lips I tasted the salt of my own tears.

RIFLE BRACED, I waded through the swamp that bordered our camp. The thieves' hideout lay at the center of the bog, enclosed by a fortress of reeds and cattail grass. I poked my rifle through the cattails, separating them enough to squint through the gap.

The criminals sat on the bank, chattering to one another as they scooped out handfuls of their creamy bounty. The powder stuck to their fingers, and they licked it off with relish. One of them threw a handful of the substance at the other, coating him in a cloud of white. The thieves formed an uneven circle around the aggressor and his victim. I clapped my hands loudly, and the activity abruptly stopped. Six guilty howler monkeys dropped Bi Trembla's can of powdered milk and scattered.

I rolled my eyes and went to pick up the canister. Tucking the powder into my pack, I waded through the swamp and back into camp. It was dark now, and most of the guests gathered at the central bonfire, listening to Tumelo tell stories or playing cards with each other. I yawned. Sometimes I liked to join them—I was a wizard at cards and loved winning money from the tourists—but today the call of my bed was stronger.

But as I passed Mr. Harving's hut, I heard raised voices. I looked down at the can, knowing I should walk past, but instead I edged closer, hovering at the back of the hut.

"Have you even written to Timothy during the whole trip?" Mr. Harving's voice demanded.

"Of course not," Kara shot back. "We're both happy to just pretend the other doesn't exist for a few more years at least."

"That's not true. He wrote to you. We got the letter in Ekwaga."

"His mother wrote it, and you know it. The handwritings were different! One person wrote the letter, and someone else signed it."

"I'm sure that's not true—"

"It is and you saw it! Just let us ignore each other. We like it that way. And it's my engagement to manage, not yours. Stop trying to manage me."

"I'm not—"

"Yes you are! You and Timothy's mother keep trying to push us closer. It's like the two of you sat down and plotted the whole thing out. Letters we didn't write. Presents we didn't send. It's all so fake."

Mr. Harving heaved a deep sigh. "Kara, we've been over this. You know I'd change it if I could, but it's the law. So let's just make the best of the situation, right? When your mother and I—"

"I know, I know. When you and Mother got engaged you couldn't stand each other, but you built an enduring relationship

60

based on respect and communication… blah blah blah. You still didn't love her, even when she died."

"That's not fair." Mr. Harving's voice took on a raw edge. "I cared for your mother."

"Care is different than love," Kara snapped. "Just leave me alone about Timothy, all right? When the time comes, I'll do what I have to. Until then just let me forget he's alive."

I heard light footsteps as Kara moved across the hut. Fearing she might emerge at any second and see that I'd overheard, I tiptoed quickly around the rear of the hut, sprinting back to camp before she could catch me.

WHEN I awoke the next morning, Tumelo stood over my bed. In one hand he held a steaming cup of black coffee. In the other he gripped the first of his morning cigars. Without bothering to lean down, he prodded my arm with the sole of his shoe. I sat up and peered out through the flap. Sunlight poured into the hut. I wondered how long I'd been asleep.

"Why are you here?" I asked, rubbing my eyes. "Bi Trembla won't let Mr. Harving go on rides until tomorrow, and Kara and I agreed we would stay at the camp today. I'm not taking another group out the first chance I've had to rest."

"It's past noon," he said, forcing his coffee into my hand so he could throw a green linen shirt to me. "Both Harvings are in my office. We're all waiting on you."

My stomach churned. I took a sip of his coffee, trying to stay calm. I'd snuck away out of fear without listening to the rest of the Harvings' conversation. What had Kara said to her father about us?

"For what?" I squeaked.

Tumelo blew cigar smoke in my face. "It seems Miss Harving has told her father about your unicorn-tracking activities. He's awake, and for whatever reason, he's decided to go along with this insane information-gathering plan of yours."

"Will you? We need both of you."

61

Coughing into his sleeve, Tumelo yanked his coffee back and washed down the cigar with a long drink. "I haven't decided anything yet. Get dressed and come to my office. I'll hear your case."

He marched out of the tent, coughing so hard it sounded as if one of his lungs might erupt. I pushed the shirt onto the floor and instead reached for the paper wrappings containing the dress Mrs. Dyer had left for me. I felt a long-dead yearning to look traditional, elegant. When I slid it on, the dress hugged my figure, a fraction tighter at the hip than fashion suggested, tying simply at the side with a set of golden strings. I smoothed the turquoise fabric down and slipped my feet into my sandals. The swish of loose material around my calves felt foreign yet familiar, like a memory retold by someone else.

Both Harvings grazed from a breakfast tray heaped with fresh fruit and bread when I entered Tumelo's office. Kara's eyes swept up my dress with appreciation. Behind her father's back, she winked at me.

Tumelo just smirked, arms crossed over his chest. "Here she is, at last," he said. "Took your sweet time, huh, princess?"

I shot him a dirty look, still too groggy to form a real retort.

Mr. Harving had lost weight. Now that I saw him sitting upright, rather than buried under rugs and blankets, I could tell how much smaller he looked. His collarbones protruded, and both cheeks looked hollowed. Now, he tried to make up for it, making sandwiches out of the bread and fruit in order to shovel more food into his weakened body. Watching him eat, I couldn't help the pang of sadness that hit me. He'd be up and on a horse by tomorrow, and my time alone with Kara would be over.

I pulled a chair from the side of the hut and sat down next to them, helping myself to some of the breakfast. Tumelo touched nothing. Despite his bulk, Tumelo usually only ate once a day. He gorged himself to capacity on Bi Trembla's elaborate evening meals and ran off the energy for the whole of the next day.

Today he breakfasted on yet another cup of black coffee. Before I left home, Mama always used to say that Tumelo's body rotted from the inside out, fresh complexion concealing the old man who lived under his skin.

Mr. Harving swallowed down his food and cleared his throat. "My daughter finally saw fit to tell me what the two of you have been sneaking around looking for. I have to say, I was shocked that you girls would attempt something so dangerous on your own. But after Kara explained to me what you saw with that stallion... well, after all our hard work, to hear about such magnificent creatures mutilated in such a way... of course you have my assistance." He looked at me out of the corner of his eye and grinned. "Just don't put me on another horse that will dump me in a bush."

We all looked to Tumelo.

My cousin calmly lit another cigar, taking his time in the typical Nazwimbe way. He put his feet up on the table. Both Harvings winced in distaste. "Let me make sure I understand you. You want us to pose as dealers. Dealers of what? What are we selling?"

"Materials," I said, through gritted teeth. He always had to be difficult. "I don't know, Tumelo. We didn't have any trouble before. Metals, probably. What else would they need from Echalend?"

"You want me to sell something when I don't know what it is?"

"Nobody is asking you to sell anything! You go in, you survey, you ask questions. And while you distract them, Kara and I will steal the moonstone."

"Steal the moonstone," Tumelo echoed. "And do what then? Bring it here? Forget about everything we've seen?"

"No," Kara said. "Of course not. Mnemba said we might write to her father—"

"Ah yes." Tumelo reclined in his chair. "Write to her father, which will take a week. Another week while he alerts the General. Another still, while the General plans what to do about it.... In this time, these men could figure everything out. They could come here. They could torch this camp or enslave us."

63

"Enslave us?" Mr. Harving spluttered, pushing the tray aside to glare at Tumelo. "My daughter and I are high-ranking members of our realm…."

Tumelo raised an eyebrow. "Do you think they care?"

I was starting to see what he was after. For Tumelo, the safety of his investments and his own person came before everything. And for me, this camp was my home. He had a point. We had to protect it. "We will steal the moonstone so they can't get any more unicorns. The sight of a newly captive unicorn terrifies people. You know it does. You know our stories. If you help us now, I will ride directly to my father for his help. No letters."

He stroked his chin, thinking.

I pressed on. "And, think about it. If all the unicorns are gone, and they expand this shantytown of tents out here, how much longer will you have custom? What are they planning to bring in on the iron road? If it's being done here, without the General's knowledge, it won't be anything you want near your business."

Tumelo sighed, swinging his feet off the table. Seeing him prepare to get up, I knew I'd won. "I still don't like it," he said. "They'll ask us questions, and we'll have no answers to give them. We shouldn't underestimate any man who can figure out how to make slaves of unicorns. You know the legends, Mnemba."

Mr. Harving tapped the table to interrupt us. "On this, I have to agree with Mr. Nzeogwu. We have to have backstory. It's a miracle you girls got through without being caught, and probably because you didn't speak to the man in charge. Let's evaluate what we know."

He took a breath, and I saw a scientist's mind at work, cataloging the situation like one of his research notebooks. "They are getting materials not native to Nazwimbe and labor from somewhere. We know how they get the unicorns. Men from Echalend can't provide them with labor. There is no official slave market here. I will go to offer them metals, and Tumelo must provide labor."

"You want Tumelo to pretend to be a slaver?" I demanded. People who enslaved their own were the lowest of the low. I wasn't sure even Tumelo could pull off that role. "It's illegal. And those who sell abroad are scum. Everyone hates them."

A smile spread over Tumelo's face, and he sat up straighter. "No, I can be a chief."

FOR THE first time I could remember, Bi Trembla looked afraid. She crouched low to the ground, stitching gold thread into the hem of Tumelo's robes while he stood like a statue. Her fingers shook as she pulled the needle through the fabric. I expected her to scold us for our rash stupidity, but she said nothing. Her eyes were fixed on her work, mouth moving without sound as she recited prayers to herself.

I stood on a stool behind Tumelo, weaving a headdress of nkombe feathers into his hair. If this was going to work, he had to truly look the part. We didn't want a repeat of the transparent disguise Kara and I had tried to pass off before.

Kara helped her father into dress pants and a jacket. Mr. Harving fastened the collar tightly and put bits of gold into holes in his sleeves. Dressed in his best clothes, he looked like I had imagined he would before they arrived: clad in tweed, sweating under the weight of his woolen overcoat. In a way, being sick helped him look the part. His muscles were less defined, and his once-tanned skin had a milk-colored paleness with twinges of green around his eyes. Like this he looked less noble, less wealthy—more apt to travel the unknown world seeking to make his fortune.

"They've seen us already," Kara said as she brushed dust off her father's coat. "We should just wear our normal clothes. If we try to dress differently now, they might grow suspicious."

I looked between the two Harvings. Although Kara had a finer build and much brighter eyes and hair, she shared her father's broad smile and pronounced jaw. If anyone studied them too closely, the resemblance would be plain. Tumelo and I looked nothing alike.

Our mothers were sisters, but where my mama was wiry with a dancer's neck and a haughty bearing, his mother was petite, round, and always smiling.

"You two will have to ride apart. And Kara should wear a headscarf or something. You look too much alike."

Mr. Harving beamed. Kara rolled her eyes.

Tumelo inspected his appearance in the mirror by the door. He turned to me, grinning triumphantly. "What do you think, Mnemba? Do I look as good as your father in this?"

The clothing suited him, and his cocky bearing and thick girth made it even more believable. But I wouldn't say that to him or we'd never hear the end of it. "You're too fat. My father has better carriage."

Tumelo slapped his huge belly. "It makes me look distinguished."

"Your father's a chief?" Kara asked, eyebrows raised. "You're a princess, then? For real?"

"Of a very small village," I said quickly. "And I'm not a princess. Our village has less than a thousand people. And our chiefs are more like mayors in your land than kings."

"Why are you here, then? Working like this?" Mr. Harving asked. I braced myself against the question I knew would follow. "If your father is a chief then you're important. I've read enough on culture here to know that. Shouldn't you be married? Or thinking about it?"

Only silence answered his question. I saw Kara step warningly on her father's foot. Mr. Harving shuffled his feet, immediately sensing he'd made an error.

After a long moment, Bi Trembla patted my back. Our eyes met, hers crinkling at the corners. "She is too good for any suitors. My girl must have the best," she said.

Something twisted in my stomach, a mix of butterflies and pain. Bi Trembla was usually so stoic and gruff, that coming from her, the words meant a lot.

"Plus she couldn't stand the thought of being away from me." Tumelo chuckled as he tied a gilded sash over his shoulder. "She's stalked me since we were children. Followed me all the way here, crying like an abandoned puppy. Admit it."

"Yeah, that's it," I said, giggling.

Bi Trembla sighed, moving about the hut and picking up Tumelo's discarded clothes. "I couldn't forgive myself if I didn't try to persuade you all to see sense once more. Nothing I say can stop you from doing this idiot thing?"

"We're doing it, Bi Trembla."

Mr. Harving laughed, rubbing the back of his head. "Two safari guides and a pair of foreigners out to the save the world. What could go wrong?"

Bi Trembla didn't even smile.

Tumelo hugged her with one arm. "We'll be home for dinner tomorrow night, *Nyanya*."

Grandmother. Tumelo had chosen his words with care, and I saw Bi Trembla's shoulders relax.

She gave a curt nod. "See that you are. If your food gets cold or you go hungry, you'll only have yourselves to blame."

Chapter Seven

SMOKE ROSE off the savanna, giving the illusion of dark volcanoes on the horizon. Thick clouds of birds flew overhead, cautioning us away, while the smoke and the song of metal beckoned. We let Tumelo ride out front. I gave directions from behind him, but trailed far enough back to show deference to his fake rank. The nkombe feathers on his headdress gleamed in the sun. Bi Trembla had done her work well. Every part of his outfit, down to the silver stars embroidered on his collar, looked like a real chief's outfit. Tumelo sat straight in his saddle, holding his reins in one hand and an ornamental spear in the other.

Beside me, Mr. Harving mopped his forehead with a wet cloth. I offered him more water from my canteen, as he'd drained his on the first part of the journey. He drank greedily, but the heat still made him sway in the saddle. I was grateful for the simple linen clothing Kara and I could wear. Today the intense sun baked our skins like clay bricks.

Tumelo glanced back at us. He grinned, but I knew him well enough to see the worry in his eyes. He tossed a few of the feathers back over his shoulder like locks of hair. "This is it. Time for my debut."

"You've been showing off your whole life," I said.

"I'm a born star," he said. "Perhaps when we're done here, I'll give up this safari business and audition for a position in the General's household players' troop."

"They'll cast you as the beast every time," I said, giggling. Tumelo put his hand over his heart, swaying as if I'd wounded him.

68

Mr. Harving loosened his collar. "I'm happy for Tumelo to take the lead role in this. The less I have to say, the better."

"The one who showed us around before didn't speak Echalende," Kara said. "Chances are good you'll barely have to say anything. I didn't."

"I think he understood more than he let on," I said. "Just be careful, okay? Stay in character the whole time. Don't assume they don't understand you."

As we reached the edge of the poacher's camp, Mr. Harving put his handkerchief to his nose. I resisted the urge to gag. In the space of just a few days, conditions in the camp had gone even further downhill. The terrible stench of rotting egg, meat, and bodies wafted over us. The smell got trapped in the humid air and hovered all around us like a putrid mist.

"My God," Mr. Harving whispered, hand covering his nose. "What is that?"

"Over two hundred men without a clean water source or a privy," Tumelo said, grimacing. He schooled his features into a frown and adjusted his position, sitting as tall and proud in the saddle as possible.

Mr. Harving rode up closer to Brekna's flanks, with Kara and I trailing behind. Kara's hair hung loose at her shoulders, partially obscuring the telltale line of her jaw.

Before we reached the worksite, two men on horses approached us. I recognized the first immediately. His thigh no longer sported a bandage from the filly's horn, but the openmouthed gaping at Kara and the hunger in his eyes was the same. Leaving his companion's side, he trotted directly over to her. He extended his hand to shake hers, but as she nervously held her hand toward him, he reached out and rested his hand on her thigh. His brazen disrespect left me speechless.

Tumelo's spear whizzed through the air. The shaft connected with the man's wrist. He reeled back with a howl, cradling his arm against his body. His companion glanced up sharply but shrugged and did nothing to intervene. That boded well. If they believed Tumelo really was a chief, no one would dare question his actions.

"What is the meaning of this?" Tumelo boomed in our language. The feathers around his face quivered when he raised his voice. "I have ridden all the way here to meet with your master, only to have one of my escort touched by the likes of you? Fetch your employer *this second*."

The two men exchanged uneasy glances. I wondered if Tumelo had overplayed his authority. When my father gave commands, he always did so with a quiet confidence. He expected to be obeyed and felt no need to raise his voice.

After a long pause, the man who had tried to stroke Kara wheeled his horse around and galloped through the mud. I had to cover my mouth to hide a smile of pure relief.

The other poacher half bowed in his saddle. He had a shrewd look about him, with narrow-set eyes and a small, pursed mouth. "Welcome. I assure you Jayweu did not mean any harm. He's not the brightest man we have, but he's fearless, and he can rope a unicorn with the best, so we keep him around." His eyes rested on Kara and me as he said, "Some servants are strong, others must possess… other talents. I apologize if he has given offense. My master is in his pavilion, overseeing the slaves' progress. I am sure he will receive you there for refreshments."

We gathered our reins to follow him, but he circled his horse around Tumelo and spoke directly to Mr. Harving. His accent was coarse, but intelligible Echalende flowed from his lips. "Hello, sir. I trust your journey to our country has gone well?"

"Yes," Mr. Harving croaked. He fanned his beet-red face. "Terribly hot here, though."

"Yes. We get that complaint a lot, I'm afraid. How did you arrive?"

"By ship, of course."

The man nodded. "Of course. What other way? Until we complete this project, that is." He gestured behind him, over the tents to the trail of smoke coiling up to the sky. "Have you spent much time in Nazwimbe? I was not aware that a new ship had landed for some weeks."

I could see Mr. Harving struggling to find excuses, so I cut in. "As you say, our client has been here some weeks. He became ill on the journey, and we had to make many stops."

The man's lip curled. "I see."

"Do you think that this is his only business?" I snapped.

The man bowed in his saddle. "Of course not. Again, I don't mean to offend."

"Are you taking us through for refreshments or not?" Tumelo interrupted. His tone did not question, and this time he didn't raise his voice. Maybe he had studied my father closely after all. "I wish to dismount and take something to drink."

"Of course, sir," the man said, switching instantly back to our language. "Follow me."

As we trailed after him toward the source of the smoke, Kara leaned over in her saddle to whisper to me. "What do you think all that was about? He seemed really suspicious."

I shook my head. "I don't know. But he speaks your language. Your father might have to do a lot more talking than we thought."

Given how much Mr. Harving had struggled to supply a simple excuse, I sincerely hoped the poacher's leader did not speak Echalende.

When we reached the edge of the labyrinth of tents and mud, Mr. Harving pulled his horse up to study the scene that played out in front of us. We watched, breath held, while two of the slaves hitched a unicorn mare to a sleigh. The mare's once proud head drooped between her knees. A hornless foal trailed her flank, ribs visible under his fuzzy baby coat. The slaves dragged the mare forward by the bridle, while an overseer whipped their backs. The animal staggered with exhaustion and the weight of the sleigh. The slaves' groans echoed through me, and despite the intolerable heat, I shivered.

I wanted to reach for Kara's hand, but the eyes of a hundred men followed us as we made our way through the camp. Even worse, her father rode beside us, and he would see everything. I wrapped a lock of the gelding's long mane around my hand instead.

The leader of the poachers reclined under a black velvet awning. He rested his feet on the back of a kneeling slave and sipped a bubbling green drink held by another. Two more laborers waved an enormous pair of feather fans above him. I squinted; the fans looked as if the poachers had simply cut off and preserved two ostrich wings. There was no sign of the black box or the moonstone. When he caught sight of our party, he rose to his feet and beckoned us toward the pavilion.

I heard Tumelo exhale. When we passed the slaves, he had slumped in his saddle, haughty bearing gone as he witnessed their abuse. Until he had seen the camp, the acting had been a game to him: a challenge for the salesman inside him to win. He'd known the risks and argued them, but looking at his face, I could tell that he only really understood everything now. An overseer whipped a slave to our left. The man's blood sprayed in an arc, spotting Tumelo's robes. He flinched, closing his eyes, as if afraid the whip might slash across his face.

Kicking Elikia forward, I rode up, even with him. His eyes were dazed. I lifted my sleeve to his face and wiped a bead of blood off his lip. Then I turned to the overseer, trying my best to sound imperious, blasé, like my mama would in this situation and shouted, "You have just splattered blood on the chieftain's robe. Clear a path."

When the man hesitated, whip still raised, Tumelo recovered himself. "Now," he ordered.

The leader craned toward us, watching our party intently, taking note of how we handled the men. I looked at Kara, and she met my eye. I could tell from the worried crease across her forehead that both of us were thinking the same thing: this was going to be much harder than last time.

We approached the pavilion. Sitting on their horse's backs, Tumelo and Mr. Harving were at eye-level with the poacher's leader. He raised his hand to Tumelo, palm flat, as was our custom when meeting a chief, but I noticed that his eyes never lowered. He watched them all the time, looking for any cracks in their image. We'd only seen him from afar that day on the ridge, but up close, I could see he was much younger than I'd imagined. His face bore no lines; his hair was ebony black. Under his velvet dinner jacket, he wore a silver belt adorned with a collection of knives.

"Greetings," he said in smooth Echalende.

Mr. Harving removed his hat and tipped it toward him.

"You're early. Or late. We weren't expecting anyone today, so you've surprised us all. If you'd sent your envoys a bit ahead, I could have arranged for someone to meet you." He smiled, revealing his teeth. None of his apology carried through in his tone. In place of his two canines were two minute silver blades. I wondered how he chewed without destroying his own cheeks.

"I was ill when I first arrived in the country," Mr. Harving parroted. His eyes darted to me, searching for affirmation. I looked away. We couldn't be seen exchanging glances like that. He was supposed to be my employer; he couldn't look to me for help.

I was glad his face still showed the hollowness of fever because the leader nodded and seemed to accept this excuse without noticing the way he looked at me. The poacher sat back in his chair and said, "I am Arusei Njenga. As you will know from our letters, I am looking to secure further labor and a steady supply of raw materials from the North. Iron, mostly. And weapons in the new style. I think you will be pleased with our progress. Already the railroad connects Nazwimbe to Erithvea and Olstwanga. All in secret, of course. It wouldn't do for our dear General to know about all this until we're nearer completion."

"Of course," Mr. Harving managed to stutter. Tumelo's hand shook on his reins.

"This part of the country is very special," Arusei continued. "Very few inhabitants, but flat. Of course, we hope that will change once we have completed our work. The General is blind. He would never give permission for a project like this. Nazwimbe needs to modernize, or we're going to be eaten alive by the countries around us."

"Very astute," said Tumelo. "But what will you do once the General finds out?"

Arusei just smiled.

While Arusei turned his attention to studying Tumelo, Kara whispered to me, "We should get water for the horses. I don't see the moonstone here with him. I don't know how long this distraction will last. We need to start looking for it. We've heard all we need to go to your father."

Arusei clapped his hands and all of us jumped in our saddles. "But come, let us go to my private tent. Take some refreshments. I have a delightful pair of dancing girls to entertain us—"

I cleared my throat and forced myself to look right into the man's cruel eyes. "My companion and I must take care of the horses. Maybe one of your men can show us where to water them?"

"Of course," Arusei said, his lips curled back a little bit too far, almost into a sneer. He flagged over two of the overseers. They were at his side in an instant. It seemed that whatever their position, everybody in the camp obeyed him as if he were a demigod. "Show these ladies where they can tend to their horses, and send laborers with fresh clothes for them to change into."

The men who approached us easily outweighed a water buffalo between them. They were each over six feet, shoulders padded with flesh and muscle. The first had a scar running the length of his face. The other smiled toward us, revealing a toothless mouth. The color drained from Kara's face, but she kept silent. I wondered if Arusei had purposely chosen these men to intimidate us.

As we followed the men away, Tumelo turned in his saddle. I'd missed some of the slave's blood: a smudge remained along his collar. I saw the fear in his eyes as he mouthed, "Hurry."

ARUSEI'S GOONS led us into a dingy stable block without windows. Cobwebs hung from the ceilings, and the pungent smell of manure hovered around us so thickly it seemed to drip down the walls. Most of the stalls were empty, but one at the back housed a pregnant unicorn mare. She turned despondent circles in her dirty enclosure, eyes glazed. Unimpressed by the accommodation, Elikia butted my arm with her head and flattened her ears.

Once they provided us with the water and grain their master commanded, the men left us in peace to seek out fresh women's clothing. They grumbled as they walked away, wondering out loud how they could be expected to find women's dresses in a camp of two hundred male laborers and guards. But I didn't think either of them would dare question their leader's command.

Left alone with the loud clamor of metal, whipcracks, and hoofbeats to drown out anything we said, I still decided to whisper, to minimize our chances of being overheard and reported.

"This is not what I expected," I said as I removed Elikia's bridle and rubbed the space between her ears. "We need to find the stone and get out. I don't know how long even Tumelo can keep this up."

"They speak Echalende. That's not good. My father isn't a good liar." Kara took a deep breath, her fingers shaking on Brekna's girth strap. "I'll never forgive myself if something happens to them."

"They'll be all right." My voice sounded shaky and unsure, even to me.

Finally I allowed myself to reach for Kara's hand. Her palm was clammy with sweat and humidity, but I pressed it to my cheek anyway. Vibrations traveled up through my fingertips, and I felt her tears begin before I heard her breath hitch.

She let out a single, unrestrained sob. Then, pinching her nose bridge, she glanced around us and choked back the rest of her tears. "Right, we know it's not in the pavilion. We can guess it'll be under guard."

"I think Arusei would keep it around him, where he can be near it most of the time," I said. "He doesn't seem the type to trust his followers with something so essential."

The unicorn mare whinnied urgently, her voice high and melodic like the stallion's had been. We rushed to over to her, peering inside her stall. The mare lay down in the dirty straw, sweat and foam drenching her white flanks. Kara yanked the bolt to her stable and knelt in the straw beside the mare. Her knees sank in the manure, but she laid her hand across the unicorn's neck anyway. She soothed her gently with soft, murmured words.

"She's foaling," she whispered in wonder. "I thought you said they could choose. Why would she choose now? Choose this place?"

I shook my head. Maybe the moonstone was affecting her. Who knew what its constant presence around the unicorns could cause? Maybe it forced the foals to come forth. If Arusei knew that, he would guard it all the more closely. The mare's sides heaved, her eyes rolling with fear and pain. Kara's hands moved to her head, massaging the stump of her horn. I crouched beside her, wincing as the smell of manure and urine intensified. The mare quieted under Kara's touch.

I glanced up toward the stall's door, terrified that the men would come back and see us touching one of their prized beasts. We had to get going. If we couldn't find the moonstone, then the entire trip would be pointless and we'd endangered ourselves for nothing. Tumelo and Mr. Harving needed us to hurry. The mare groaned, body shuddering with pain. I couldn't just leave the animal like this.

"You haven't picked your time too well, girl," Kara said, reaching under the mare's long, matted mane to scratch her neck. "You don't want to have your baby in this place. Keep him inside you, shelter him from what this will be like for a little bit longer."

The unicorn looked into my eyes, and I saw something I'd never expected to see in the eyes of an animal: understanding. She held eye contact in a way no horse would and rested her head against my calf. In that moment, I felt entirely connected to her by an invisible force. The mare's body convulsed.

"Here, swap places with me and stroke her head," I said. I had some experience in delivering horse foals. My family raised many types of animals, and I'd grown up running through the fields after the playful foals and baby goats. I remembered assisting my father with the broodmares in the early hours of the morning, holding the torch close so he could see. If I could align the foal's legs inside her, I could help the mare in her delivery.

"Yes, Doctor," Kara said with a mocking salute. "Nurse Kara Harving reporting."

I chuckled, kneeling behind the mare's hind legs. The squelch of manure and the fluids from the mare's womb was enough to make my stomach churn. I gagged but forced the bile back down. I stroked the mare's flank gently to relax her. No creature should have to give birth in filth like this.

Wincing, I slid my arm into the unicorn's tight birth canal. This foal was definitely her first. The mare groaned. I could feel the sharp edges of impossibly tiny hooves brush against my fingertips. The baby was too small. The hooves felt smaller than a dog's paw. *Why now?* I questioned the mare in my mind. *You could have held him for another year if you had to.*

I pulled gently on the foal's limbs as the mare pushed against me. Her contractions were so strong—I feared she would shatter my wrist—but I maintained the pressure anyway. The foal slipped downward, his hooves and ears sliding out of the mare.

With a final heave, the mare pushed her baby out onto the dirty straw. I immediately snatched him up, pulling the placenta off over his head and rubbing his coat to stimulate the blood. He was the size of a mountain dog puppy, too small to even reach his mother's udder if she stood up. But every other part of him was perfect, from his white, bearded face and inquisitive ears to the tip of his blunt baby horn. The delicate foal took his first breath, and I pressed his mouth to his mother's teat, letting him guzzle the nourishing first milk.

The mare lifted her head to look at her foal while he suckled. She whinnied at him and the baby gave a soft nicker in reply. Her eyes met mine again for a split second. Then she groaned again. Her head dropped into Kara's lap, but her eyes stayed open, unblinking. The foal shivered in my hold. The mare had known exactly what she was doing when she decided to give birth now. She had chosen the only moment she could to give her baby a chance at escape.

"She gave him to us," Kara said, echoing exactly what I was thinking. She leaned down and kissed the mare's dusty forehead. Then, without a hint of squeamishness, she reached for my blood-covered fingers and squeezed them.

"Do you have a shawl in your saddlebag?" I asked. She nodded and rose to fetch it. Her linen pants were stained with blood. I looked down at myself. I was drenched in red from my chest down, bits of gooey placenta stuck to my trousers. The blood had started to dry on my arm, sticking to the hairs and forming a crust. Together, we'd look like a pair of roadside murderers.

I wrapped the foal tightly in Kara's wool shawl, fashioning a sack to drape over my shoulder so that I could carry him easily. How we could look for the moonstone now, covered in blood, carrying a newborn unicorn, I didn't know. But when I was a child, and my grandfather succumbed to palsy, the Mkuu told me that the last wish of the dying gave special powers to the living that watched his soul depart. We could only pray that the unicorn's last wish would see us and her baby safely back home.

Chapter Eight

WE SQUEEZED the remainder of the unicorn's milk from her teat into Kara's canteen. It felt wrong to milk her like this, like we were violating her body by prodding and gripping her still warm udder while she lay dead beside us. But we had nothing else to give her baby. After dipping my fingers into the warm, opaque liquid, I let the foal suckle drops from my fingers while Kara held him. His toothless gums tickled my hands, but the baby seemed to know he was tiny and fed greedily, butting into the soft flesh of Kara's bosom whenever we stopped feeding him.

"It's gotten quiet outside," Kara observed. I pulled my fingers out of the foal's mouth and listened. She was right. The sound of men's work had dwindled to a low murmur, and I could no longer hear the shouts of the overseers or the cracks of their whips.

A gunshot fired. The sound ripped through me, and the terrible image of Tumelo lying facedown, bleeding in the mud forced its way into my mind. I pushed the foal fully into Kara's lap and scrambled to my feet.

Stumbling out of the stable block, I peered around the corner into the yard. Rows of slaves lay facedown in the mud, the overseers walking around them, counting. Several of the poachers raced toward an enormous black velvet tent with thick red silk hangings. My stomach sank. That tent could only belong to Arusei.

I stepped back into the stables, motioning Kara to stand up. We had to get out quickly, before any of the other men came for us. There was no way we could know if Tumelo or Mr. Harving had just been shot. But if they had been discovered, our only chance to save them now was to find the moonstone and get to

79

my father as fast as we could. If we failed to get the moonstone, Arusei could lure dozens more unicorns in the time it would take us to return. If we managed to escape, Arusei might become desperate. Who knew how many more of the creatures he would capture in order to speed up the building process. Only General Zuberi would have the forces to take on Arusei's men. We had to get the moonstone, because once he completed his iron highway and brought in whatever he planned from the North, even the General might not be able to stop him.

"We have to go," I hissed. "They're all running toward a huge tent on the ridge. It has to be where Arusei took your father and Tumelo."

Kara cradled the foal against her chest. "We can't just leave them here! We don't even know if the gunshot is related to them. It could have been a slave running away, for all we know. Get your gun. Let's go. We'll go see what's happened and take them with us."

I shook my head. "If the stone isn't in the pavilion, I'd bet it's in the tent. Maybe one of them found it and that's why this is happening. We need to make a distraction, get the stone and go. But we don't have time to saddle all the horses, and even if we did, how far could we ride before they caught us? We have to bring my father."

"How can we leave them? Especially if one of them just got shot? How can you think about stealing the damn stone right now?"

"If someone shot them, they're already dead. There's nothing we can do for them now if that happened." My jaw tightened. The image of Tumelo lying dead flashed through my mind again, and I fought to stay focused while everything about the new life I'd been building seemed to crumble away. My training in how to stay calm during an attack on safari took over. I focused on what we had to do. I looked through the bars of the stables, at the unicorn mare's lifeless corpse, and an idea formed.

Kara stared at me disbelievingly. "How can you say that?"

"Tighten Brekna's girth and get on him," I barked, racing out of the stable block again. I knew she would resent me for belting out commands, but there was no time to explain.

I whistled toward the remaining overseers. "The unicorn!" I called, waving my arms about, demanding their attention. "She's foaling. Come quick! I think the baby's stuck. If we don't do something now, the birth will kill both of them!"

The overseers exchanged glances, seeming to deliberate whether it would be worse for them to disobey whatever orders their leader had given them or to let two of Arusei's prized unicorns die. In the end a throng of them sprinted toward the stable block as I ducked back inside. Though Elikia wasn't wearing her bridle or saddle, I'd ridden her enough times to know she would look after me without them. I threw open her stable door and vaulted onto her back. Kara sat on Brekna, as I'd asked, but her arms were crossed over her chest and angry tears spilled down her cheeks.

The overseers raced right past our horses and into the end stall that had held the unicorn. Seeing her still body, and the blood, they began shouting at one another, arguing over whose responsibility it was to cut open her belly and rescue the foal inside.

With Brekna following closely behind, I nudged my horse and she sprinted forward. Kara continued to glare at me, jabbing her heels angrily into Brekna's sides. She wore the foal slung over her shoulder.

We burst out of the stable block at a gallop. My hands gripped Elikia's long mane to stay aboard as my seat slipped on her sweaty back. Arusei and a handful of his other men had appeared at the front of his tent, squinting down at the stable block to see what had happened and who was yelling. None of them carried rifles. I couldn't see either Tumelo or Mr. Harving among them.

Sudden fear made me abandon any plan to race away. Tumelo wasn't there. He could be lying inside, choking on his last gasp. I changed directions, and we charged toward them, our horses devouring the distance in a few easy strides. At first I think Arusei expected us to stop, dismount, and come inside to see the famous dancing girls perform like he promised us. He stood waiting, his hands on his knife belt, a patient, half-bemused smile on his face. Only at the last second did he or his men see the blood on our clothes and understand that neither of us intended to slow down. All they could do was leap aside as we galloped directly into the ornate tent. My foot connected with a tentpole, and half the structure came down behind us, sealing the entrance.

The inside of the tent was almost empty, but in the middle of the floor stood a cage. It was gilded with gold leaf, but the bars were of solid iron. Tumelo and Mr. Harving sat inside it, naked flesh of their backs pressing against the bars. Both of them had been fully stripped. A trail of blood flowed from Tumelo's lip down his chin, and a puffy bruise already swelled below his eye. An equally ornate chair sat directly in front of the cage, gold and encrusted with gems. I covered my mouth. The throne reminded me of even more stories from my childhood—of kings who used to rule all of Nazwimbe and half the surrounding territories beside. Those kings harnessed the mythical battle-fever of the unicorns and used them to drive chariots of fire. I swallowed. In those legends, the kings had possessed a moonstone, with powers never seen before or after, that drove the unicorns into frenzy. I swallowed. Those things were all just stories.

"How?" Mr. Harving gasped when he saw Kara, his eyes scanning her from head to toe, taking in the sight of her bloodstained clothing. "Are you injured? What happened?"

Kara shook her head, tears coming too fast for her to speak. She held up the foal for her father to see. A ghost of a smile appeared on Mr. Harving's face.

"We heard gunshots… we thought maybe one of you…," I said. I paced around the cage, looking for a way to open it. The small door at the side was bolted fast with a series of padlocks. I rattled them uselessly, looking around the tent for the key. "How were you caught? What did he ask?"

"He knew when we arrived it was wrong," Mr. Harving said, shaking his head. "When he brought us up here, he had his thugs strip us and throw us in here. Tumelo tried to fight them off, so they hit him."

"Mnemba." Tumelo cut Mr. Harving off. His voice was overly firm, the way he often sounded right before he ordered me to clean out the latrines or scrub down the stable block. I braced myself against whatever he was about to say. Elikia shifted nervously underneath me. "You have to get out of here—now. If you stay here and get caught, we're all dead. We're stuck in here. Get your father. That's the only chance we have."

"The moonstone," I said, staying rooted on the spot. We couldn't leave without it. Not if there was any chance that the legends could be true. From the looks of things, Arusei believed that they were. "Have you seen it? Anywhere in here?"

"Look at the chair. The stones."

Outside I heard men shouting and the fabric of the tent shuddered. A knife blade pierced the fabric sides. We were running out of time.

My eyes scanned over the gilded chair again and rested on the seat. Directly under where Arusei would sit was an enormous opaque moonstone, polished and fitted to the chair as if the throne had been designed to house it. I flung myself down from Elikia's back. I slid my nails into the crevices along the moonstone's outline. It lifted easily from the chair, leaving behind a crater of gold. Hastily, I buried it with our clothes in Brekna's saddlebags.

"We'll come back," Kara promised her father. Snot and tears made tracks down her dirt-stained cheeks.

"Go," Mr. Harving said, settling back against the bars again. He looked at me, eyes glassy with resignation. "Take care of her."

Tumelo grimaced at me through the bars. I reached in and grasped his arm, knowing he would break if I cried too.

Holding to her mane for my life, I kicked Elikia, and we charged through the fabric at the rear of the tent. I heard rattling of bars behind us, scaring the horses forward. I wrapped my arms around my mare's neck, and we galloped away, never looking back.

ELIKIA'S HEART beat so fast her ribs shook against my legs. Sweat from her back soaked through my trousers and foam dripped down her dark chest. My own legs felt like mortar, heavy and impossible to move, molded to the mare's shape. Beside me, Brekna and Kara gasped for breath. Steam rose from the stallion's wet back. The unicorn foal struggled in the shawl, whinnying to be fed.

As soon as we'd burst from the tent, Arusei's men had tried to chase after us. But our horses were too fast and well fed, and even the smallest of the poachers outweighed us by stones. I'd lost track of how many miles we'd galloped across the savanna, weeds tangling around the horses' legs as they ran. I'd made sure to lead us across rivers and dry soil, to make us harder to track. Now that we had reached the road, our tracks would blend with the well-trampled path, and we could finally afford to slow down.

"How far is it? To your father's village?" Kara asked, her voice coming out as a dry rasp. We needed to find water, for ourselves and the horses.

"A few hours from here, still," I wheezed. "We'll need to stop and find water. To drink, give the horses a break, and clean ourselves up if we can. If someone sees us on the road, they'll have us arrested with all this blood all over us."

Kara glared at me and then looked away, mouth set in a tight line. "We should never have left them like that, and we deserve whatever happens now. We should never have asked them to go. What were we thinking? Thinking we could just go into a poacher's camp and get information like a couple of amateur detectives."

She looked out over the savanna behind us, grinding her teeth.

"Hey," I said, halting Elikia so I could look her in the eye. "Don't talk like that. We're going to get them out of there."

"They're probably dead already, like you said they would be. What use does Arusei have for them? And it's our fault."

"What chance did we have to free them on our own? We didn't have the key to that cage, and you saw how fast those men came after us. Besides, if Arusei was going to just kill them, he would have done it. Not strip them and lock them in a cage. He's using them to make sure we come back."

Kara shook her head, shutting her eyes. Tears leaked under her lids. "Me and my stupid adventure."

That stung. I bit my lip and tried not to show how hurt I felt. "It's not your fault.... He wanted to do it. He knew what he was getting himself into."

"He never would have even known about if I hadn't insisted on going on that stupid stakeout. I've been so self-centered. All I wanted was to have a bit of fun before he forced me into marrying Timothy, and now that might have killed him."

I looked away from her, unable to listen to anything else she might say. A bit of fun. A stupid adventure. Her comments played over and over in my mind, growing more painful every time I repeated them.

Tears welled up in my eyes but anger helped me blink them back. I had been so stupid to allow myself to get attached to her. She was a tourist. I'd known the whole time she was leaving, and this was temporary. And what could I offer her anyway? If every time she tried to kiss me, to pull me to her, I pushed her away. But to hear her say it like that made it real. She dismissed me like a round of cards or a horse race.

"So have I just been 'a bit of fun' to you?" My heart trembled, but my voice was firm.

"What else could you be? Even if I wanted something else, I'm not allowed to have it. I have to marry Timothy. It's the law. And because I selfishly tried to just forget that, now my father is imprisoned by a crazed warlord, and I might never see him again."

"I thought you might like me," I spat. I felt petty for thinking about myself, considering what her father and my cousin were going through, but the words and feelings tumbled out. "So I'm the stupid one."

"I do like you!" she shouted, sweat-soaked hair falling across her face. The sleeping unicorn foal's head jerked up. "But what can come of that? Look where it's got us so far! I can't afford to let my feelings stretch any more than that."

The fire of anger cooled into a sadness in my chest. She liked me. She'd actually said it. But she was right. What could come of it? I folded my arms across my chest, wishing I had the courage to reach for her. Kara bit her lip. It was so chapped by dry wind and heat that it started to bleed.

I pushed Elikia another step forward, so that Kara and I sat parallel to one another. Gently, I swung my leg over Brekna's flank and settled into the space behind her saddle. The horse sighed at the extra weight but stood still. I took a deep breath as Kara's body tensed, and I half expected her to push me away. Instead she closed her eyes, and I slipped my arm around her waist.

In Nazwimbe, we have a saying: what has been sealed in blood cannot be undone. The bond between a mother and the child she conceived, a murder, a rape, the cut of a vicious whip… all these are actions that no one can take back. When I pressed my lips to hers, tasting the salt-iron sweetness of the blood on her lip, I knew there was no going back for me.

One way or another, I'd find a way around the laws that bound her to her fiancé. I needed to be more than her one adventure. I needed her to help me heal.

I FILLED my canteen and let the horses have a long drink from the stream before I stepped into the freezing water to wash myself. Kara fished through our saddlebags for extra clothes to put on. We'd packed extra linen clothes for Tumelo and Mr. Harving, so that they could change out of their hot formal attire the second we left Arusei's camp behind. Wincing, I watched her pull out Tumelo's favorite, sky-blue tunic.

"Wear that one," I urged as I scrubbed my arms. I didn't want to wear Tumelo's clothes or let her wear her father's. People's scents always had a way of lingering inside clothes. Knowing Tumelo, the fabric would be perfumed with essence of cigar whether it was clean or not.

She nodded and pulled the tunic over her wet hair. It fell to her knees, and she tied it at the waist like a dress. Taking a seat by the stream, she watched me wash with a small smirk. "You should ride naked. Like a goddess."

I snorted. "Right. Ride naked all the way to my father's house."

"We could stop again before we get there." Her eyes gleamed with mischief, and I was so happy to see any emotion in them other than pain that I almost agreed to her ridiculous proposal. I imagined the look Mama would give me and smiled. But the thought of washing horsehair out of my private regions made me shake my head. There are some places fur should never go.

I went to the saddlebags myself and pulled out Mr. Harving's spare clothes. He'd packed two sets of trousers and a green cotton shirt. I pulled out the smaller of the trouser pairs. The moonstone sparkled beneath the pile of linens. I tucked it back into Kara's remaining shawl and tugged Mr. Harving's trousers up my legs. They swamped my body, but at least they were bloodless and nobody who passed us on the road would fear us as criminals.

On the other side of the stream, a male grelbok lowered its head to drink. It looked like an antelope but more delicate with a light, arid build. The grelbok fed on minerals in addition to grass, its body processing them and using them to build elaborate horns of gold and aluminum. They were more elusive even than the unicorns. I'd never managed to find one before. I moved slowly, so that it wouldn't run, and pointed the creature out to Kara.

"It's good luck, to see those," I said. "At weddings, a man dresses up like a grelbok and dances. Sometimes he hides in the bushes and bursts out later to scare the drunks away. Seeing a real one is supposed to bring good luck for life."

The grelbok raised its horned head, white muzzle twitching as it sniffed the air. It stood and watched us, cocking its head as if something about our smell confused it. The unicorn foal whinnied.

"Well good," Kara said, taking my hand. "If we're going to rescue my father and your crazy cousin, we need all the luck we can get."

Chapter Nine

THE SUN started to set again by the time we reached the outskirts of my home village of Sagadi. I leaned down to unlock the perimeter fence that surrounded the village. A chest-height structure made of overlapping wooden planks, it kept the cattle and sheep enclosed and some of the lesser predators out. The lock was a simple iron fastening. My father welcomed all human travelers openly.

As I closed the latch behind us, an old gray sheepdog jumped up, barking and licking at my feet. His tail wagged so hard his entire body shook. Grinning, I looked around for his owner. A gangly goatherd came racing toward us, staff raised, his goats bleating as they trotted after him.

"I'm so sorry, miss," he said, batting the dog away. "He's not usually so overfamiliar with strangers."

"Have I become a stranger, Jelle?"

The goatherd lifted his hand to his eyes to shield them from the sun and squinted up at me. Then a smile split his face. "Mnemba?"

I grinned, leapt down from Elikia's back, and embraced him. Our town had less than a thousand people, and as the chief's daughter, I knew everyone, or at least, I used to. Jelle was a year older than me. As a child, I used to spend whole afternoons chasing him through these fields while his father and brothers minded their goats. Always, Grapf, his shaggy gray shadow, accompanied us.

He swung me off my feet, and then he rubbed the back of his head. "Sorry, Mnemba. I know I should be more proper with you being Chief Adebayo's daughter. But it's been ages…. I started to think I wouldn't see you again."

I clapped his shoulder. "I know. I've been away a long time."

"I don't blame you for having to get away. At least that bastard's getting what he deserves now." He glanced up at Kara, eyes widening at the sight of her.

Occasionally, a spice merchant with white skin might pass through Sagadi, but I could count the times that had happened in my lifetime on two hands. Usually, our townspeople had to take their things to a bigger village to trade. After working with Tumelo and our tourists for over a year, it was easy to forget how strange it must be for people in remote Sagadi to see someone who looked like Kara. And even I had never seen a white woman with hair the color of hot copper and cerulean eyes like hers.

Jelle tipped his head to her and lifted his palm, holding it up flat. Kara nodded back to him but then looked to me in confusion. I chuckled and said in Echalende, "That's a gesture of respect and greeting. Jelle is a friend of mine, from when I was a child."

Kara lifted her hand and tried to mimic Jelle's movement. "How do I say 'it's nice to meet you,' in your language?" she asked.

"*Nimefurahi kukutana nawe.*"

She repeated what I told her, her tongue slipping awkwardly over the foreign words. But I loved her even more for trying. Jelle's grin got bigger.

"Well," I said, giving him a final squeeze. His body felt so warm and solid, anchoring. "We're in a rush, and we need to speak to my father. It's been too long, Jelle. I missed you."

I jumped back onto Elikia, and we trotted quickly through the grazing lands, passing through herds of sheep, goats, and cattle. Their herders looked up as we passed. Some failed to recognize me in my strange clothes, accompanied by a foreigner. They watched us with suspicion, while others scanned my face and waved, huge smiles cracking their faces. I knew everyone. Every face. A lump formed in my throat. Even after what had happened, this place was home, and I should have visited long ago.

We rode through rows of crops next, our pace slowing as Kara investigated plants she didn't know. She plucked leaves and lifted them to her nose to absorb the scents. The aroma of citrus and mint filled the air. All the crops looked strong, green. Sagadi wasn't a rich village. We didn't have silks or imported furniture like they had in Mugbani, where the General resided. But what we grew, we shared, and no one ever went hungry. I noticed that in a year, many of our corn and plantain fields had been replaced by tall sugarcane stalks. If that continued, the people here would soon see more of foreigners who looked like Kara.

On the other side of the farming fields, we came to a square, fenced on all sides. Two wells stood in the middle of the square, guarded by two of my father's finest warriors. My lungs suddenly contracted like I'd breathed in a mouthful of water. I looked past the wells to the road. He was there. All I wanted was to turn and gallop away. Before I could stop her, Kara jumped down and took Brekna's reins, leading him toward the fence.

"Kara, stop!" I called.

"Why?" she asked, mouth quirking into a scowl. "Brekna needs more water. Elikia could probably use it as well. Why is the well guarded? Doesn't everybody need to use it? Do you ration it?"

"It's not a well for water," I whispered.

"Ah," Kara said, putting her foot back in her stirrup and hopping aboard again. "Oil? A coin hoard? Some people in Echalend keep their money underground too."

I swallowed, closing my eyes. "We call them The Pits of Regret. They're prisons."

Kara's mouth gaped. "Prisons? You keep human beings down there? In those small wells, in the dark?"

I nodded, unable to say more without my voice breaking. I cast a glance over at the pits, chewing my lip.

"For how long?" Kara demanded. "Those wells don't even look big enough for a person to lie down. How long do they stay there? For what crimes?"

I braced myself as a familiar crawling sensation spread over my stomach and abdomen. If I'd learned anything about Kara in the last few weeks, it was that her questions wouldn't stop unless I gave her some answers. "Only blood crimes can you get sentenced to the Pits: murder, rape, assaults that permanently maim or disable. We have them in all our villages and cities in Nazwimbe. Things like theft or not paying taxes, we give whippings or fines. How long they stay in there depends."

"On what?"

I took a long shuddering breath. Why was she pressing me like this? Couldn't she tell how uncomfortable I was? "The people they've wronged. When someone is sentenced to the Pits, they must stay down there until their victim or their victim's family decides to forgive them."

"For a blood crime… who would forgive them? That's a life sentence, right?" She cast her gaze back over at the wells. "Years, at the least."

I shrugged, avoiding her eyes. "Once a year, we lower a dagger. Then the prisoner must choose: wait another year in hope of forgiveness or take his own life and end his suffering."

She studied my face and her hand went to her mouth as a shock of realization seemed to wash over her. "The man who attacked you… raped you… is he… is he down there?"

I nodded, pressing my lips together. "He is, or he was. It's been over a year now, and I don't care to ask whether he lives or not."

Kara sighed. "We'll be on our way, then. And I won't ask anything about this place again. I'm sorry."

One of the guards watched us closely, and before we could ride away, he raised his arm to stop us. Chief's daughter or not, when flagged by a warrior, I had to stop. If we moved on without hearing what he had to say, then for the protection of the village, he was allowed to throw a spear or use a crossbow. At the distance, he probably couldn't see my face anyway. He wore a mask of wood, with a solemn frown painted on it in white and red. A beaded fringe hung across his eyes. On his right hand, he wore the ceremonial weapon of our people: five metal blades attached to rings, worn like claws extending over the fingernails. My eyes locked on those blades and my whole body went rigid.

As he approached us, he removed his mask. I remembered his face but not his name. He raised his hand in respect. "Mnemba. I haven't seen you in months. Passing through or do you have words for our prisoner?"

"I have nothing to say to him. And we're in a hurry. We need to get to my father as fast as possible." I gritted my teeth. I should have expected this.

The guard nodded. A heavy silence passed between us. My attacker's actions had split the village apart. Before he became the beast who raped the chieftain's daughter, the monster who ripped my stomach and savaged my womb with the blades on his fingers, Obasi had been a warrior. He smiled often and let young boys try on his mask and wave his spear. The village had loved him. Try as I might to forget it, there were some in Sagadi who still did and who held on to the hope that I would forgive him.

Unbidden, Elikia trotted forward along the road. I wasn't sure if she sensed my need to be away or she had started to recognize the land and was beckoned by the grains at home. Whatever the reason, I felt a wash of gratitude to my horse. I mentally promised her all the corn she could hold when we reached the house.

EVEN THOUGH I'd tried to tell her otherwise, Kara still held on to the idea that I was some kind of princess. To her understanding, a chief was a ruler. And in Echalend, as my tourists had told me over and over again, rulers lived in palaces of marble with the largest, fanciest streetlamps of all. As we reached my family's home—a long white oval building with a roof of thatched sugarcane, surrounded by a daub fence and a flurry of chickens—Kara crinkled her nose in surprise. Although larger than the wooden huts most of the villagers owned, our house was not ornate, and we didn't have any lamps—fancy or otherwise.

The foal whinnied and butted Kara's arm. "He's hungry," she said. "And his mother's milk has run out."

"Behind the house, we have a stable with about twenty broodmares," I said, dismounting again to undo the latch on the gate. Like the town's outer wall, we had only a simple fastening to keep the animals inside. "I don't know if his stomach will handle horse milk, but that's the closest I think we can come by. I'm sure at least one of them will have a foal at heel. He's so tiny he won't need much."

As I pushed the gate, the front door to the house swung open. A tall, slender woman stepped outside. She raised one hand to shield her eyes from the sun, peering down the garden path toward us. My heart beat faster and I gnawed my lip, hiding a smile. *Mama.*

Leaving Elikia by the gate with Kara, I sprinted up the walk toward her. Her narrow-eyed look of suspicion transformed into a giant smile as I approached. She spread her arms wide, and I threw myself into her embrace, inhaling the scent of flour and daffodils.

"Mnemba," she breathed, pushing me back to kiss both my cheeks. "What a surprise… a good surprise…. Tumelo finally convinced you to come back home?"

I swallowed. "In a manner of speaking."

"Is he here with you?"

"No."

Mama peered over at Kara, scanning her from to head to toe, her eyes gradually widening as she took in the girl's appearance and the unicorn foal slung over her shoulder. She raised a carefully plucked eyebrow. "Something tells me this isn't just a social visit, is it?"

I shook my head, suddenly not trusting myself to speak.

For the time being, she let me off the hook. Mama braced her hands on her hips and beckoned to Kara. She immediately spoke in Echalende as soon as Kara was within earshot. "You'd better come in, then. Turn the horses out back. You're in time for dinner. Your father is in the kitchen, mixing up some of his famous strong ale—I think Imrai is helping him. I've got a whole chicken roasting in the oven, so there will be plenty."

Despite the welcome in her words, Mama's face was guarded, her stance rigid. She wanted me to come home out of desire to see my family, not because some disaster had happened at the camp.

"I'll bring the horses out back," Kara said, looking at her feet. I could tell she felt out of place, unwanted. "I'm sure I can figure out where they go. Go spend the time we have with your family."

I nodded. It would be easier to break the news to my father without her there. I didn't need anybody else to witness the scolding I was sure would follow. Years of ruling our village had taught my father a deathly calm. He never raised his voice or displayed his anger, but somehow could manage to make me feel the size of an ant.

"We need milk for the foal," I said to Mama. "He's an orphan. I'm not sure if horse milk will do, but it's the closest thing I can think of."

"The strawberry-colored mare had a foal last week. She's producing more than enough milk for two. After we eat, I'll collect some of her milk for you girls to feed him. If that doesn't suit, we can try the goats. How did you stumble across a baby unicorn?"

"It's all part of the story, Mama," I said, closing my eyes tiredly.

Kara gave my arm a squeeze and then led the horses away behind the house. As soon as she was out of earshot, Mama exploded. "I don't know what's going on, but if you've brought a girl like that all the way here, without Tumelo, I have a feeling it's not going to be good. You both look exhausted. Like you crawled off your deathbeds. How bad is it?"

"Bad. Really bad." My voice wavered and tears fell down my cheeks.

She wrapped me in her strong arms again, sighing. "Come inside. Whatever it is, your father will know what to do. He always does."

I followed her in, removing my boots at the door, breathing in all the smells of home: roasting chicken, fire smoke, fresh fire-baked bread, and the basket of new flowers Mama always kept full on the table in the kitchen. The woven rugs of corn husk felt scratchy against my feet, now that I'd gotten used to the furs and cotton rugs of the South. Everything looked the same as when I'd left, even though it had been a year. My grandfather's weathered elephant statue still stood in the hall; the mellow green painted walls were still scuffed and marked. My father was in the kitchen, our main room, shaving a ginger root into the clay pot on the table.

Even with all the tourists I had met, Adebayo Ohakim still was the largest man I had ever seen. He dwarfed Tumelo, standing over six and half feet, with a broad chest and arms that bulged with muscles the size of melons. He wore feathers woven into the long black and gray braids on his head. His green chief's cloak was slung over a chair in the corner of the room, and for now he wore a simple linen tunic. He held my baby brother, Imrai, balanced on his hip. The toddler chewed on a corn husk. Another wash of pain filled my chest. At two and a half, Imrai had lost most of his baby roundness now. While I was away, he'd transformed into a little boy—a tiny copy of my father with the same skin, coffee-dark and smooth, with long, curled lashes. He wouldn't even know who I was.

When he looked up, Father dropped the ginger root and immediately placed Imrai on the floor. He bit his lip. Like me, he always did that when he was trying to stop himself from showing too much emotion.

"Where have you been?" The question was harsh, but his voice was gentle.

"You know, around," I said and edged over to smell the ginger ale inside the pot. "Smells like a good batch."

He nodded and lifted a stirring spoon full of the warm gold liquid to my lips. "Go on. You were always my toughest critic."

I took a sip and coughed. "Too much yeast!" I gagged.

My father chuckled and rubbed the back of his neck. "I let Imrai decide how much we'd put in." He bent down and picked up the toddler again. "Can you say hello to your sister, Imrai?"

The boy batted his eyelashes at me. He had light gray eyes like my mama, uncommon in Nazwimbe. Mine were dark, like my father's. His face held no trace of recognition, but he obeyed my father anyway. "Hello, sister."

I reached for him, and he shrank away back into my father's neck. Adebayo shrugged. "He'll come around, once he gets used to seeing you again. It's good to see you, safe and whole."

Mama made her way into the kitchen and sat on the edge of the table. "Safe and whole... interesting choice of words, Ade. It might interest you to know that there is a foreign white girl behind the house, carrying an orphan unicorn foal. And Tumelo didn't come with her."

My father frowned and passed Imrai to Mama. She took the boy out of the kitchen and into the large bunk-bedroom we all shared. He tilted my chin up to look at him. He sighed, as if noticing the puffiness of my eyes and the greenish circles around them for the first time. "What's happened?"

I collapsed against his chest, and the words spilled out like water.

When I finished telling him about the poachers, the unicorns, and Tumelo's capture, he shook his head slowly. "I can't believe you would be so reckless. I expect that kind of thing from Tumelo—he's always been rash and silly. But we raised you to take more caution and to think before you try something so stupid. How did you think you could possibly get away with something like that? If they're smart enough to make a railroad without the General's knowledge, they're smart enough to catch a couple of teenagers. I know Arusei from years ago. Now I'll have to clean up your mess."

When tears started to fall down my cheeks again, he softened. "It'll be all right. I think you're right to say that if Arusei wanted Tumelo dead, he would have just shot him. He's holding him. They'll be nervous now, knowing you got away and hoping that you'll come back to get them. At least he doesn't know who you are. Tonight, we'll feed you up, let you sleep in your own bed. All you need to focus on is getting to know your brother again." He brushed the tears away from my face with the edge of his thumb. "You look too skinny. Tumelo's working you too hard. When we get him out, I'll have words with that boy."

I snuggled deeper into his chest, wishing that I was still Imrai's age and still believed that my father's arms could make everything better. While his hold still comforted me, it had lost its magical ability to heal a year ago.

"We'll ride for the capital in the morning," he said. "Why don't you bring your friend inside?"

I released my hold on him and went to find Kara. As I put on my boots, my father appeared behind me at the doorway. "And Mnemba, when this is all over, don't let it be another year before we see you again."

WE ATE dinner in near silence, nibbling at the spiced chicken my mother had prepared. I watched Kara struggle to eat without a knife or fork, the way we did here. After each bite, her greasy fingers hovered in the air and she looked down at her lap in confusion, as if willing a napkin to materialize from nothing. The foal nestled on the floor close to her feet, happy and bloated now that we'd fed him half a bucket of mare's milk. My parents spent the meal exchanging looks, a silent language only they understood. Only Imrai seemed at peace. He made mountains out of his potatoes and galloped imaginary fig horses across his plate, chattering to my mother with his mouth stuffed.

Father didn't speak any Echalende. Before they met, Mama had once worked as a secretary in the capital, taking records for the General. She had taught me snippets of the language as a child and Tumelo had helped me get better. I knew my father didn't want to offend by speaking Nazwim around Kara and my mother wouldn't want to make my father feel ignorant by showing off her Echalende. So instead none of us said anything, sitting in straight-backed silence.

"This is very good," Kara said, tentatively breaking off another piece of the tender meat. She held it up and smiled, so that my father could catch the gist of what she was saying. She lifted the unicorn foal from the ground into her lap. "If it's all right, I'm going to take him outside and feed him again."

"I'll help," I said, rising from the table before Mama could say anything to stop me. I knew the foal might not be hungry again, but I'd take any excuse to leave the table with her.

We went out behind the house, and I followed Kara into the stable block to the strawberry mare's stall. I recognized her as one of the first horses I'd ridden as a child. She'd been young then, and frisky. Too wild for a little girl, Mama had complained. But Father thought riding wild ponies turned children into formidable adults. I soothed her and played with her inquisitive foal's ears while Kara pressed the unicorn directly to her teat to suckle.

"It's nice, seeing your home," she said, pulling the unicorn's nose back to make him feed more slowly. Surprisingly, he was ravenous again. "I wish it wasn't under these circumstances, and I'm sure your family does too, but still, I like it, seeing where you come from."

"Even with the language barrier?" I teased, leaning over to plant a soft kiss on her forehead. I wanted to kiss her lips, but so soon after our encounter with the guard at Obasi's well, I couldn't. "My father barely speaks a word of Echalende. Sorry. It's not like tourists really come here."

Tentatively, Kara reached out to stroke my hair. Even though I wanted her to touch me, I stiffened as her fingers wound themselves around a loose braid. An image of a large hand grabbing my braids and throwing me against the ground flashed through my mind. I pulled back and braced myself against the barn's wall.

"I'm not going to hurt you," she whispered, a sad frown tugging at the corners of her mouth. "When will you realize that? Sometimes you're okay and then you back off again. You don't have to keep pushing away from me."

I traced her jawline with my finger. Her sadness made me feel guilty, even though I couldn't help the way my body was reacting. "I think it's just... seeing the Pits today. Knowing he's so close."

"What do you think will happen? Will he kill himself?"

I shrugged. "They all do in the end."

"But what if it takes years? Is he going to haunt you for that whole time?"

"I try to think about other things. It helps when I'm away from here, working. I love my family, but it's worse every time I come here. When it first happened, my father never really got it. He kept saying again and again, 'We caught him, we caught him, it's over.' He didn't understand why the rest of me didn't heal when my cuts did."

Kara adjusted her position so she could lean up against the wall beside me. She looked up toward the barn's rafters. "We need to get Tumelo back."

I nodded. Our shoulders brushed. The accidental touch disarmed me, and my body relaxed. "What do we do about the stone?"

"Give it to the General?"

"I'm not sure... we have these legends. I was always taught that they were stories, just fairy tales. But they talk about a moonstone that can be used to stir the unicorns into battle fever. They respond to it, and it makes them vicious. Kings used it."

She slowly rested her head against my shoulder. "So it's more than just a way to lure them. It changes their behavior."

"If the legends are true."

The foal struggled to be put down. We carried him outside the mare's stall and let him try his legs on the solid earth. His legs splayed, and he shuffled around the inside of the barn, nosing curiously at stray wisps of hay and empty buckets.

Laying down in the clean straw, we watched our quadrupedal little orphan explore his world on wobbly, bowed legs.

Kara stroked my stomach as I breathed in the scent of fresh cut straw. "Do you trust the General with it? If it turns out to be everything the legends say it is?" she asked.

"I don't know."

"Then for now, we keep it close."

Chapter Ten

MAMA LIFTED Imrai to the assembly bell, helping him swing the ceremonial gong with his chubby toddler arms. Someday, calling the warriors' gatherings would fall to him, and by the time he was a man, Mama wanted Imrai to feel like his exercising his power was as natural as taking a breath. When he finished ringing the bell, he waved at me in excitement. I'd made friends with my brother again by slipping him cubes of sugar at breakfast when Mama's back was turned.

The village warriors drew around my father in a semicircle, pulling their masks down over their faces. Our central square filled with the men and their tall horses. They wore thick paint smeared across their chests in jagged scratches of red and green. Each of the twenty men had a rifle slung over his back, and wore the ceremonial claws covering their right hands. They presented themselves as a deadly mix of new technology and formidable dedication to tradition.

I struggled to climb into Elikia's saddle, my legs restricted by the fabric of the new dress Mama had given me and forced me to wear. It wouldn't do for me to appear before the General dressed in dusty man's clothes like an ill-bred tramp. Kara and I parked our horses behind my father, facing the crescent moon of assembled warriors.

I felt out of place in the warriors' gatherings with so many of Obasi's friends and former brothers appraising me like an enemy. In Nazwimbe, when you were elected to the warrior's guild by the chief, the position was for life. The guild became your family. Before I left with Tumelo, I had told my father how I felt several times, but he always dismissed me. *They understood,* he'd comforted, *they knew that what Obasi did was unforgivable. It's all in your head, Mnemba. When will you stop believing the whole town is your enemy?* But if that was the case, then why did I always feel like they waited for me to do something? Like their eyes held hope, pity, and accusation all at the same time?

Tumelo was the only one who understood, who had listened to me and noticed how differently they treated me after it happened. He'd come back from his studies at the guide's academy in Mugdani and had found me a shell of the person I used to be. *Come with me, cousin,* he'd said, his eyes bright. *Let's see if we can put some spirit back inside you.* I closed my eyes, listening to the sounds of the gathering horses and the roosters crowing the early morning. We had to get him back, whatever it took.

"One of our own has been taken," my father began, raising his voice to a loud boom. All the men assembled already knew what had happened to Tumelo. My father had sent out runners the night before to make sure that all of them would be ready to leave at daybreak. But the announcement, the stirring of suspense and blood rage by the chief's speech—these were our traditions. Mama stepped behind him and settled his headdress over his dark braids. "My nephew and a foreigner who was his guest have been taken captive by a slaver's group who would overthrow our beloved General."

The warriors raised their clawed hands into the air and chanted, "We follow you."

"You honor me," my father replied.

At the noise of the bell, most of the villagers emerged from their huts, rubbing their eyes. They raised their fists sleepily, some of them covering yawns. A naked toddler ran out into the street, and his mother chased after him, grabbing him in her arms and belatedly raising her fist with a rueful grin.

Kara leaned over to me, so close that her soft hair brushed against my cheek. Mama had given her a new bag to hold the foal.

He nipped my shoulder playfully when she drew close. "What are they saying? Doing?"

I shrugged. "It's a ritual. We always do it before the warriors leave the village. Back before Nazwimbe was all one country, and the chiefs used to fight each other, it was a promise between the chief, the warriors, and the town's people that we were all bound together. Now it's just tradition, and my father likes to continue it."

Mama handed Father his chieftain's spear, and he raised it to signal the warriors to file out. She blew me a kiss and lifted Imrai so he could wave us off. Kara and I rode up alongside Father, with the men following behind us. I felt their eyes boring into me, and I wished we could go to the General without the ceremonial guard. General Zuberi commanded a force of men larger than the total population of our village. He didn't need the warriors Father brought to ride out against Arusei, but for a chief to greet his overlord alone signaled disrespect.

As we rode down the path, I could hear the dissenting murmur of conversation growing louder behind us. My father's eyes remained in front, and he seemed not to notice the way a few of his warriors traded glances as we rode past the Pits. Fury bubbled in my chest, and I remembered once again why I had followed Tumelo and left the only home I'd ever known behind. What Obasi did had broken me, but it was the town—these men—who finally drove me away.

"What's wrong?" Kara asked. She didn't bother to whisper, but I doubted any of the warriors spoke her language anyway.

I ground my teeth and looked toward the Pits. "It's like they all blame me. I mean, I know that everybody accepts it was Obasi's fault... but still, whenever I come here, it's like people keep expecting me to forgive him. Because he was a paragon. Because he wasn't a bad person, before. Because he was their friend. They don't understand that it's not about them, and it never has been. It's one of the reasons I don't come home anymore."

Even though he couldn't understand the language, my father understood the anger in my tone. He turned in his saddle, pulled his horse up, and rode next to me. Following the direction of my gaze, he squeezed my arm and said gruffly, "I know what you're saying, Mnemba, and how you feel. And I know that before you left home, I didn't try to understand. Now I wish I had listened better about how some of the people here made you feel. Until Obasi takes his life, and he will, there are always going to be people who wish it was different. People hold out hope that the past can be healed. But the weight of this doesn't have to rest on you anymore. Know that if in a moment of weakness, you give in and that animal ever claws his way out of the earth, I will be standing there to gut him."

Emotion made me speechless. Silence fell behind us. I chanced a look back. The men who had been whispering stared at my father with gaping mouths. A few of the other warriors bore a smile that surprised me.

The man nearest to us looked between my father and me, whispering, "What's bound in blood cannot be undone."

Pain and hope both swelled inside me.

Father looked toward the Pits and spat on the earth.

AS WE approached Mugdani from the height of the mountains, the whole city seemed to move like a stream of multicolored water beneath us. I hadn't visited the capital since I was a small child, and seeing it with fresh eyes took my breath away. The streets were paved with polished bronze. The oblong houses of the ministers and top military officials lined every road, painted in brilliant reds and blues, the tiles of their roofs glittering like a fish's scales. Terraced farms lined the mountain's sides, holding stalks of wheat and corn that billowed in golden wisps. Mounted warriors manned every street corner, their masked faces impassive while children, merchants, and aristocrats scurried past them.

I wondered what kind of weapons Arusei planned to bring in from Echalend that made him think he could overthrow a General who governed a place like this. No wonder he needed the unicorns.

The General's villa stood on a man-made hill at the very center of Mugdani. It was positioned so he could watch everything but live well above the noise and smell. As we descended into the crowded streets, Kara covered her nose with her hand. The city's perfect image was shattered by the stench of human sweat and animal manure.

Everywhere we rode, eyes turned to stare at us—at Kara. In a city full of ministers, the people were used to seeing processions of chiefs with their entourages come to petition the General. But a white girl with red hair, carrying a tiny unicorn foal, riding a stallion that lived to show off, drew their attention, and people came to the front of their shops and stalls to stare. Brekna danced under her, snorting. The stallion knew when people were watching him, and he thrived on their admiration. Tumelo would have been proud of his horse's display.

"He's feisty today," Kara panted as she tightened Brekna's reins. "I expected he'd be exhausted by now, but he's going to unseat me if he doesn't stop bouncing around."

"He's excited. It's not every day huge crowds of people come out to stare at him. Plus he knows he's got a rider worth showing off." I winked at her. Her cheeks were already pink from the sun, but she blushed as red as a hogfish snout.

"All the tour companies and shipmen told us we couldn't go to Mugdani. Even diplomats meet the General outside the capital, usually," she said. "I might be the first person from Echalend to ever see it."

That explained the reaction of the crowd. Children were now lining up along the streets to point at us. The guards squirmed in their saddles.

My father scowled at the attention. He motioned to the rest of the warriors behind us. "Let's trot the rest of the stretch. People are getting too curious, and I don't want to get stuck in a mob."

We trotted to the base of the General's villa complex, scattering merchants like minnows ahead of us. Some of them raised their fists and cursed as they quickly wheeled their carts out of our way. The odor of manure and bodies was replaced by the fragrance of cinnamon, orange peel, and nutmeg as spices fell onto the street. A lump formed in my throat. Those smells reminded me of Bi Trembla's baking, and I wondered what she must be thinking now. Tumelo had promised her we would return by nightfall, but I hadn't dared ride for the camp before going to my father. If Arusei's men had tracked our horses home, I didn't want to think about what they might have done to Bi Trembla. Especially if they believed she was hiding us.

Five guards stood watch over the cobbled path that led up the mound to the General's residence. My father raised his hand flat to greet them and then bent in his saddle to answer their questions. Unlike the rest of the warriors on the streets, they didn't wear masks. Their brown eyes swept accusingly over Kara, and they pointed, tone angry. But they kept their voices so low I couldn't make out all the words they said. When the name "Arusei" passed my father's lips, the guards exchanged uneasy glances and stepped aside. I was suddenly curious how my father, and everyone else, seemed to know of him.

General Zuberi met us on the terrace outside his red brick villa. He looked nothing like the proud warrior I remembered from my childhood. His back had stooped, and he walked with a cane. An attendant followed closely after him, clutching a folding wooden stool in her hands. She set the stool up for the General, and he lowered himself onto it with wobbling knees as our party filed into the courtyard.

He had never been a large man, but when I was a child, people used to say that the General was like a leopard. Not so big as a lion nor as bloodthirsty as a hydra, but when he struck, he moved unseen, dragging his enemies by the throat to their deaths with such grace people never even saw the slaughter. Even now, old as he was, when he sat, his posture had a rigid straightness, and he balanced his cane across his knees like a rifle.

He looked up at my father and his weathered face cracked into a smile. "Ade! It's been too long, my friend. What an honor... and a surprise."

Father raised his arm in salute and then climbed down to greet the General. They grasped forearms, and then the General peered over my father's shoulder. His eyes narrowed, and he stood up again, limping toward Kara.

She removed the hat Mama had given her to block the sun, a gesture I knew was meant to show respect in Echalend. The General leaned his weight on Brekna's sweaty flank and spoke in Echalende. His accent was thick and musical and his words gentle, but I was suddenly aware of the predatory intensity in his eyes. All at once he definitely didn't look fragile or old anymore, and I wondered if we should have left Kara with his guards at the gate. "My dear, you're a long way from home."

"We're here about your cousin, Arusei," Father said. "He's building a railway and planning to bring weapons from abroad."

The General abruptly turned away from Kara. His eyes snapped up to my father's face. "Where did you get this information?"

"My daughter."

Everyone turned to me.

I swallowed as General Zuberi turned his intense stare on me. "I work as a safari guide now, for my cousin in the lower delta. I was out with one of our guests—Miss Harving, who you see there—and we came across a pile of unicorn horns, thirty of them at least. It's not normal... they don't shed their horns or live in groups."

"Come to the point," the General urged, tapping his cane on the ground.

"Arusei and a group of men are capturing the unicorns. We followed them to their camp. They're building a railroad, as my father said. And they have my cousin; they took him captive. And Miss Harving's father. They're going to bring weapons in on the railroad."

"And they just let you waltz into their camp to have a look? Did you see these weapons? Arusei just told all of this to you?" General Zuberi raised an eyebrow.

I flushed, having to repeat it yet again made me realize just how foolish and naïve we had been. "No, sir. Initially, we tracked them back to their camp to see what they were doing with the unicorns. One of Arusei's men saw Kara and assumed we must be dealers from Echalend. Then we went back, and her father and my cousin met with him. But it all went wrong, and he arrested them. We only just managed to get away. We dressed my cousin up like a chief and Mr. Harving as a weapons dealer."

Father chuckled, rolling his eyes despite the situation. "I bet Tumelo loved that."

"And you have stolen one of Arusei's beasts, I see." General Zuberi gestured toward the tiny unicorn. He reached up toward Kara. "May I see it? Satisfy an old man's curiosity—I've never seen one so small or so close."

Kara unwound the bag's straps from around her neck and passed the baby to the General. In the arms of a new person, the foal began to struggle, but he was firmly enclosed by the fabric. The General ran his fingers over the fuzz-covered horn. "How did he capture you, huh? Was it a moonstone?"

"We didn't see what he used." I swallowed, glad his eyes were fixed on the little animal instead of me. I couldn't have the most powerful man in Nazwimbe believing that I had lied to him.

"Did you see the weapons? Do you have any idea what it is that he plans to bring or what we will face?"

I shook my head. "The railroad is not complete yet. But they've taken hundreds of slaves. I don't know where they are getting them. I believe they are capturing townspeople from local villages or offering money to their chiefs in exchange for delivering them."

My father made a sound like a growl in the back of his throat. His warriors fidgeted in their saddles. The excesses and greed of many local chiefs had been stamped out when General Zuberi took power, but Father took reports of this behavior personally. In our village, we had people who had sought refuge from the tyranny of their own chiefs, many with amputated limbs and smiles scarred by blades.

The General continued to stroke the foal's baby fuzz. The unicorn gradually relaxed under his touch, sucking on the man's gnarled finger as if hoping his new friend might feed him. Zuberi's attendant crept forward unbidden and positioned the stool so that the General could rest again. "My mind keeps returning to these creatures. Arusei has wanted to take power for years. He believes that I'm too old and that the chiefs have too much autonomy. The railroad is worrying. Arusei has always looked to the North for help." He cast a glance up at Kara. "One of the reasons we do not allow foreigners here, is so that they can't map our capital. But the use of the creatures, why? It seems like a lot of trouble to go through. Yes, they are powerful, but horses are easier to come by and elephants are stronger. Why these specific animals... unless they are needed for more than building. I fear whatever weapon he plans to bring into this country."

"We should act quickly," Father said, crossing his arms over his broad chest. "Arusei doesn't have that many men yet. Although he has slaves, I doubt they will fight for him, especially if they see their General and know they have a chance to get away."

General Zuberi passed the foal back up to Kara. He stroked his chin and one of his legs tapped the earth as he thought. "It will take me a few days to give orders to the commanders here. I can be ready to leave in two days' time. Until then, you will have a place here as my guests. Your men will be housed comfortably in city lodgings, and you can take up residence in the guest's cottage at the base of the mound."

"Two days?" I demanded, ignoring the sharp look my father gave me. "Tumelo could be dead in two days." If he wasn't gone already…. "Can't we leave today? It's still early, not even noon. If we left now, we could reach the poacher's camp by sunset."

The General scowled. "I was not asking for your input, Miss Ohakim. I know my armies and my commanders. We will strike at dawn, not at night when our torches will let them know we are coming. Without more information on the weapons, we must do it that way. I have been a military commander longer than you have been alive. I am sorry that your cousin is a prisoner, but if you had come to your father first, instead of foolishly trying to infiltrate a serious criminal operation, you would not have these concerns. Dismount. My attendants will see to you."

My face went hot with shame.

He raised an arm and a herd of servants, hiding in places I'd never noticed, appeared in the courtyard. Each of them was dressed in simple black shifts with a red scarf wrapped around their heads. Zuberi made his own way inside, leaving us in his servants' capable hands. I dismounted, my dress clinging awkwardly to the horn on my saddle.

As soon as my feet touched the ground, my father grabbed me by the arm and shook me. "What possessed you to speak out to the General in such a manner?"

I pulled my arm away but could still feel the places where his fingers had been as I cradled it against my chest. "Tumelo. Even if Arusei doesn't kill him, who knows what he is doing to them right now? The sooner we get them away, the better."

"Do you think I like the idea of my nephew languishing in that traitor's cage? I hate it. But the General will want to do things thoroughly, not rush in and hope everything works out," he hissed. I looked away. We had rushed in, and it had cost us, but part of me worried now that the cost of moving too slowly might be worse.

One of the General's attendants approached and took Elikia's reins from my hand. She moved to take the foal, but Kara held the bag against her chest and shook her head. Another servant raised her hand and spoke in Echalende, "The ladies will come with me. I will show you to a room and a hot bath. We apologize that you will have to share. All three of the General's wives are in residence at this time, but General Zuberi does not feel it appropriate for you to stay in the warriors' barracks."

As we turned to walk away, my father pulled me to face him. He leaned down and pressed a warning kiss to my cheek. "I expect to find you still here when I return tomorrow."

THE ATTENDANT led us to a room at the back of the General's enormous villa. For me, having my own hut with a bed and a bath at Tumelo's camp had seemed like a luxury after a lifetime of sharing a room with my family. This room had a bed framed in gilded iron, large enough for a whole family to sleep on a single mattress. A fire roared on the hearth, bathing the space in warm, orange light. A basket of fruits lay on the side table, piled high with guavas and bananas. The floors were covered with plush velvet rugs in blue and silver—the General's war colors. At any other time, I would have rolled into the bed's feather softness, enveloping myself in the crisp new sheets. Instead, I just stared at the basket of fruit and wished I were back at the camp, swiping bruised mangoes from Tumelo's cracked bowl.

"I should take the animal to the stables for you," the attendant sniffed. "He will make a mess of the room. The only beast we keep in the house is the General's pet phoenix."

"We'll clean up after him," I promised. I didn't want the foal or Kara to panic.

The servant raised her arm stiffly and backed out of the room.

"Well, this is a beautiful prison," Kara said when the attendant shut the door behind her. "I understand that the General wants to be cautious, but two days? Who knows what could happen to them in two days."

I nodded and flopped over backward onto the bed, looking up at the blue ceiling. "That's what I tried to tell the General. As you saw, he didn't listen. He'll leave when he chooses to, no matter what I say to him."

"So is that what we're going to do?" Kara took the foal out of his bag and let him wander the room. He licked one of the guavas and drew his head back in disgust.

"You don't think rushing into things has gotten us into enough trouble already?"

The foal lost his balance on the slick wooden floor, slipping and bumping his chin. He whinnied miserably, drawing his spindly legs under his body. Kara knelt to help him back to his feet, bracing him with her hands so he didn't fall again. "I can't live with myself, sitting here, doing nothing, while those thugs might be torturing my father. And you can't live without Tumelo."

I hesitated, picking at a stray thread on the bed's cover. If we left now, Father and the General would be furious. Arusei could catch us sneaking around his camp again, and once he had all of us in his clutches, what was to stop him from killing us? By the time General Zuberi arrived with his forces, we could be dead, and if we weren't then Zuberi could very well have us horsewhipped for disobeying him. Being a foreigner wouldn't save Kara from the lash. I shuddered. The whip would shred her soft, creamy flesh, leaving her back a pulpy mess like the inside of a fig.

My father's scolding rang in my ears. We had been rash and stupid. "What will we do once we get there?" I asked. "If they're alive, they'll be locked in that cage. And you can bet Arusei will keep the keys on him."

Kara shrugged. "What will we do here? Just sit here and worry? Arusei has thirty armed men at the most. Why does General Zuberi need two whole days to get ready?"

"He probably wants to make sure he can give a real show of force. To put others off the idea of trying something like it themselves."

"And what about the legends? With the way you lied to the General out there, we can hardly tell him now, 'oh look, we mysteriously stumbled upon Arusei's moonstone'—if he's made a weapon out of the unicorns, shouldn't we find out? Shouldn't we *warn* them? If the General marches straight into a death trap, what will happen to Tumelo then?" When she widened her blue eyes at me, I couldn't decide if I wanted to kiss her or strangle her before she could tempt me into any more trouble. "We won't ride up and investigate. We can find a place to watch, and if we get the opportunity to free them, we take it. Otherwise, we can map out the area. And if there is nothing we can do, I promise we'll wait for General Zuberi to arrive."

"You know we could get whipped right? I'm not saying we will, but it's illegal to disobey a military order." I swung my legs off the bed and went to stand behind her, tracing my fingers along the perfect curve of her spine. She shifted, turning toward me to return my affection. Before I could think about stepping away, her arm snaked out, wrapping itself around my buttocks and pulling me to her with sudden aggression. But for the first time, I felt my body yield at her forwardness, my stomach pressed against her.

"Where I come from, we'd get shot."

I shivered. Barbarians. "The whippings aren't something to laugh at, though… some people's backs never recover."

She looked up into my eyes. "I know you want to protect me, but I know what I'm getting myself into. We started this. We can't let your father walk straight into a trap too."

Chapter Eleven

FOR THE second time in a week, I found myself staging an escape before the sun came up. We tiptoed through the villa, holding our shoes and trying to remember how to get out of the enormous house without opening the door to General Zuberi's bedroom. As we crept through the kitchen, I imagined Zuberi greeting us at the door—feet bare, rubbing his eyes to clear the sleep, using his rifle as a cane. The moonstone weighed heavily in the pocket inside my shirt. It would be too easy for him to take it from me.

The unicorn foal wasn't helping my nerves, but Kara refused to leave him behind. Although he was currently sleeping in his carrier bag, belly full of mare's milk, there was no way to tell him he had to be quiet. If he woke up and started whinnying, we'd be in trouble.

"This is insane," I whispered as Kara wedged the front door open a crack. My feet kept moving, even as I protested. We slipped through the opening and left the door slightly ajar, too afraid to risk the sound of closing it. We were going to get caught before we even made it down the hill, which was just as well, maybe, since I was still working on what to tell the guards and the stable master. At least if we were caught in the house, maybe we could invent a believable excuse.

Kara nodded but didn't stop as she half skipped down the path to hide behind a tree. I studied the ground beneath us, following the line of hoof prints leading away from the courtyard. I motioned her back over, and we jogged along the line. My heel came down on a sharp rock, and I had to stifle a yelp, hopping a few steps and biting down curses.

General Zuberi's stable block looked like a small village. Enclosed by a low wall, the stables were made up of a collection of brick buildings, each larger than my family's house. The buildings bordered a courtyard with a well and an exercise arena. A pair of stable boys stood on the edge of a stack of millet, sorting it into piles to distribute to the animals.

We hugged the tree line, sneaking around the boys in a wide arc. My heel was bleeding, leaving drops of blood on the gray gravel.

"We're never going to find our horses down there. That place is huge, and if we hang around looking for them, we'll definitely get caught," Kara said as she ducked under a low-hanging branch. "I say we take the first two we find and go."

My mouth hung open, and I glanced sharply at her to see if she was joking. She crouched low against the tree, not even looking at me. Steal horses from the most powerful man in Nazwimbe? Now I knew she'd lost her mind. Perhaps grief and fear had driven her insane. And what did that say about me? Since I was still following her.

"We can't steal from General Zuberi! Are you crazy?" Even if we only found one of our horses and had to ride double the whole way, it would be better than stealing from a warlord.

Her hand reached back and found mine, giving it a squeeze. She turned to me, a strange gleam in her eye—I couldn't decide if it was insanity or mischief. "You said yourself there are only three penalties in Nazwimbe: whipping, fines, or the Pit. We haven't committed a blood crime, so they won't throw us in a well. And we're already disobeying a military order, so we'll probably already get horsewhipped like you said. I'm sure your father will get the horses back later. So, what else do we have to lose?"

The rest of our skin, an extra quart of blood, our dignity, our reputations—fuck it. Tumelo was worth all of that. I sighed and then nodded.

We snuck into the first of the stable buildings. In the flickering torchlight, I peered over stable doors to consider the horses inside.

While Kara scanned the stalls, I looked around for our own horses. The barn was quiet, and I wasn't going to add theft to our growing list of transgressions unless we absolutely had to.

A low, metallic moan echoed through the barn and a pool of blue, outdoor light flooded into the stable block.

"Someone's here. Stop arguing with me. Pick a horse and let's go!" Kara urged, tugging me closer to the stalls.

Small, perky white ears poked out from above the first door, and a playful child's pony nipped my shoulder, kicking at his stable door to be fed. In the next stall over, a chestnut roan nibbled the top of the unicorn foal's head when Kara backed too close to him. The baby let out a shrill, irritated whinny.

"These will have to do," Kara said, grabbing the bridle on the peg next to the roan's door. She unlocked the door and thrust the bit between the pony's teeth, vaulting aboard. The pony was so round that his stomach wobbled when she nudged him. Her feet hung down to his knees.

The white pony bit me again, and I cursed. Riding a miniature beast with an attitude problem into a savanna full of predators was not part of the plan. Not that we'd had much of a plan to begin with. And with the way things seemed to be going, these brats probably belonged to the General's granddaughters. The morning just got worse and worse. I could almost feel the whip against my back.

I snatched the white pony's bridle and went into his stable. He stomped gleefully and turned circles in his enclosure. I seized him by the muzzle, glaring deep into his playful stare to let him know I was not in the mood to play. The pony lunged, intent on nipping me on the thigh. As soon as his mouth opened, I shoved the bit into it. The little horse stilled in surprise.

I climbed aboard. His back was broad and he felt more solid than I had expected. Kara pressed the roan forward and the white pony followed on instinct. I grabbed a handful of his long mane to steady myself against his short, choppy gait.

When they saw us cantering over the gravel, the two stable boys dropped their pitchforks and ran after us. Something about the way the ponies accelerated, ears pricked forward with delight, made me think that this was not the first time they'd been chased. I wondered how often they escaped without riders. The stable boys began shouting, and I heard doors opening behind us as servants and guards stumbled out of their huts.

Kara did not lead us down the gravel path like I expected. Instead, she galloped into the wooded gardens, making use of the ponies' small size to weave in and out of trees. There was only one gate. The rest of the complex was surrounded by a low fence, chest height at the most. I gulped, knowing exactly what she was planning to do.

We galloped downhill, reaching the base of the mound in minutes. The wall loomed ahead, looking much larger than it had the day before when I'd looked at it from the height of Elikia's back. If the pony stopped, his neck was too short to catch me. I'd sail over his head alone and break my neck on the wall.

"Kara, no!" I shouted too late.

With a gleeful snort, the pony took off like an antelope, tucking his delicate feet against his enormous belly. He cleared the wall by a foot, bucking triumphantly when his hooves touched the ground on the other side. I nearly slipped off his round sides. Kara pulled up next to me, face wind-whipped and flushed.

"That was *brilliant*," she breathed.

Brilliantly crazy. Brilliantly stupid. Her lips crushed against mine.

IN THE quietness of the early morning, the rest of Mugdani seemed like a ghost town. The throngs of merchants still slept in their beds, and the warriors who guarded the street corners hadn't yet come to their posts. No children lined the roads to stare at us as we cantered through the empty streets.

After their mad dash to freedom, the ponies were already struggling for breath. They were soft and unfit, used to an easy life with too much grain. We had no choice but to stick to the main road as we left the city behind. I didn't know the area and couldn't hope to guide us back to Arusei's camp from here. All I knew was that if we headed east along the road, we would pass through towns I recognized. Then I could find my bearings again.

For now we had no choice but to gallop. Even as the ponies started to wheeze, we had to press them forward until we reached the mountains surrounding the city. The valley itself was flat and dry, and we needed somewhere to hide.

The General's guards would chase us. Zuberi would never let us just gallop to freedom on two of his horses without at least trying to stop us. Especially when he'd specifically ordered us not to leave. If we'd been riding our own horses, we could have used the advantage of our lead, staying ahead of them until we reached lands I knew. Then we could have disappeared by following the rivers. But on these ponies, we would struggle. Their strides were too short, and we were too heavy.

At the base of the mountain foothills, I spotted an abandoned set of farms. The fields were overgrown and the thatched roofs on the huts were black with decay. Many of the local farmers had moved into the city or out into the neighboring plantations, where they could earn more money.

I pointed to the buildings. "We should hide there and wait until the General's guard passes us. Once they've gone past, we can follow the road for a few miles east, until I can figure out how to lead us away through the brush."

We trotted across the weeds and long-dead stubble of crops. Old straw covered the floor of the first hut, and I decided to tie the ponies there to let them rest. I gave the white terror a few handfuls of water from my canteen, wishing the farm had a trough or a forgotten bucket we could use.

Kara rubbed circles on the roan's forehead. He leaned into her in exhaustion, cheekiness completely drained out. Now that she was on the ground, the foal's eyes snapped open. He struggled madly in his carrier, wanting to stretch his legs. I tried to pat the white pony's neck, hoping his nastiness had dwindled. He rewarded my kindness by biting my elbow and trying to stand on my foot.

I shook my head, rubbing the welt forming on my arm. "If this pony belongs to one of the General's granddaughters, she must be pretty brave. He's tried to bite me about twenty times."

"Or he's a one-person pony and wants you to know it. In case you get any crazy ideas about keeping him."

"No chance. I'd swap him for a pack mule," I said. I tied the pony's reins to a post on the inside wall, double-knotting the loop, just in case he tried something in our absence. We left them to rest and walked to the next hut, settling ourselves down in the deep straw, beneath a crack in the daub wall.

The gap was just wide enough that I could squint through and see the road. I rested my back against the wall. Kara sat down in the straw beside me. Her cheeks were still red with excitement; her feet tapped against the straw. I could almost feel the sparks of her nervous energy buzzing against my skin.

She cleared her throat. "I wanted to tell you… if it were an option, if I wasn't already engaged… I would stay here with you. I just thought you should know that. In case something happens to one of us."

I leaned over, biting my lip to suppress a smile, and stroked her hair back out of her face. "Nothing's going to happen to us." I settled for providing comfort because I couldn't say that I hadn't given up on trying to keep her. How could I tell her everything I hoped, when so much of it seemed impossible?

Kneeling up, she straddled my legs, chest pressed against mine. Her whisper tickled my ear as her lips brushed against the lobe. "And I wanted to thank you. For doing this. I know we'll get in trouble. And I know I coerced you into looking for the unicorns before…."

I lost track of everything she was saying as she nibbled the base of my ear. Her fingers crept up my shirt, pressing her nails into the flesh of my back. The sensation hovered dizzyingly on the edge of pain. The feeling brought the memory of Obasi's claws, but instead of feeling panic, it made me want her more. Obasi's scratches had bled; when he'd held me down he had wanted to maim me, mark me as his, ruin me for anyone else. This pain, dull and delicious, was simply primal, natural. I pulled her shirt off and pressed my mouth to the sweet dough of her flesh.

As she slid down my body, I heard the echo of hoofbeats clambering down the road and managed to peer through the crevice in time to see the General's guard clatter past. Her fingers stroked the skin of my thighs. She clamped her hand over my mouth, silencing the catlike noises passing though my lips. I gripped the wall, anchoring myself to something real.

A KNOT of dread and guilt formed in my stomach as we rode up the dusty, red lane. I wanted to swap horses for something we could escape on, should the need arise, so I'd led us back to Tumelo's safari camp. The afternoon bonfire flickered at the center of the camp, the dark clouds overhead strengthening its glow. In Tumelo's absence, Bi Trembla would be holding court over it, filling the guests' heads with stories from her childhood.

The white pony's head drooped between his knees, his ears flopping sideways like a donkey's. By the time we stumbled into camp, I didn't even have to touch the reins to pull him up. We halted in the shadow of the fire. When I dismounted, the poor creature didn't even have the energy to nip me. Instead, he leaned part of his weight against my side.

A shadow passed across the firelight. I looked up to see Bi Trembla scurrying from her chair. I longed to bury my sorrows in her ample bosom, but if I considered our history, she was more likely to slap me than give me a hug. I sighed and braced myself for impact.

Her hand connected with my cheek. I yelped and Kara winced.

"Where have you been?" Bi Trembla panted, tears welling up in her eyes. She spoke in Echalende, so Kara understood every word of my humiliation. "I have been thinking the worst for days. Wondering if you all died out there. Of all the inconsiderate things you've ever done, this—" She stopped and looked around behind us. Her voice rose in pitch, and she clutched her chest. "Where is Tumelo?"

"Captured," I squeaked.

Bi Trembla closed her eyes slowly. "How did it happen?"

"They didn't buy any of it. When Kara and I went to stable the horses, they were taken. We only just got away ourselves."

"Why didn't you come to me immediately? Tell me what had happened, instead of letting me believe some poacher put a bullet through all of your heads?" Bi Trembla reached out and slapped my other cheek, but her this time, her touch was light.

"I didn't want to lead them back here!" I took a step back, out of her arm's range. "We went to my father, and then the General—"

"And where are they?"

I squirmed. "Still in Mugdani… the General needed time to prepare before he rides out. The poachers are heavily armed."

Bi Trembla's hawk eyes scanned over the tired ponies she didn't recognize and our lack of supplies. She looked into my eyes with an intensity that made me feel like she was scanning my soul. "And the General knows you are here? Whose horses are those?"

I looked at the ground and mumbled, "We snuck out."

"You *stole* General Zuberi's ponies?"

"It was my fault, Bi Trembla," Kara interrupted, moving so she stood between us, blocking me from further violent onslaught. "I begged her to go. My father was captured, and I need to know if he's still alive. I'm sorry for the worry we've caused you, but since you've spent the last few days thinking that we were dead, perhaps you can imagine what it's been like for me not knowing if my own father—my only living blood relative—is still alive."

Bi Trembla stared at Kara, and for a moment I was afraid she might strike her as well. Instead, she reached out and cupped Kara's chin, sighing. "I can't imagine, child."

While I was glad she hadn't slapped Kara, I still couldn't help thinking how unfair it was. Tumelo was my blood relative too!

The housekeeper looked over to the fire and called for one of the kitchen boys. After thrusting our horses' reins into his hands, she took both of us by the upper arms and steered us toward the fire. "I don't like what you are about to do. You nearly got caught before, and it would be prudent to wait for the General. But I understand. At least let me feed you before you ride off again."

STANDING ON her gelding's back to reach the lowest branch, Kara scrambled up the trunk like an oversized, redheaded baboon. She swung herself into the canopy and disappeared into a cloud of dark green leaves.

I stood on the ground and fanned the small pit fire I'd built to keep the predators away, wondering just how I was going to replicate that feat of gymnastic athleticism when Kara's head popped out from the green. "Come on," she urged, waving at me from above. "It's not hard, just stand on the horse's back and pull yourself up."

"How did you get to be the master climber?" I grumbled. I felt self-conscious being the one stuck on the ground, worrying, when I spent hours every day riding out. But heights had always made me nervous. "Weren't you a proper young lady in Echalend?"

She chuckled, swinging from a branch with one hand. "I used to climb out of my window all the time to go to political rallies. Father was okay with what they were saying, and with me reading all the literature, but he didn't like the idea of me going to those parts of the city. I had to get back in the house somehow."

"Check and make sure there aren't any leopards up there before I come up."

Her eyes widened, and I swallowed down a giggle.

"Did you see tracks?" she demanded, lowering herself back down to the first branch. "Do you think there could be one, higher up, waiting?"

"Sometimes they lurk right at the top, waiting for the monkeys." I couldn't hold back any longer and my face split into a grin.

Kara scowled and gently kicked the top of my head. "Get up here."

Sighing, I dragged my horse under the branch, mounted, and swiveled so that I faced toward her rump. I stood shakily and crouched on her haunches. The mare gave an irritated swish of her tail. I swallowed hard and reached for the branch above. I caught it and dangled, struggling to pull my leg over. Kara grabbed me and helped me the rest of the way up.

I nestled against the tree's trunk, adjusting the dials on my binoculars until Arusei's camp blurred into view. We were close enough to the camp to see what was happening, but if we stayed hidden in the trees, they would struggle to see us. I'd chosen our spot with care: a small forest enclave surrounding a watering hole. Kara had reluctantly left the foal to Bi Trembla's care. If we got caught now, neither of us wanted him returned to captivity.

I looked out over the sea of tents and mud. The railroad's tracks extended almost to the camp now, and I could make out square patches of dry earth where tents had been moved to make more space. Squinting along the iron river, I saw something that made my insides swim. A great steel machine the size of two bull elephants rode proudly along the track, steam and smoke billowing behind it. The engine had a grate of metallic teeth that flashed in the light, and it ate up the tracks at breathtaking speed.

As the machine slowed, the overseers began to drive teams of laborers toward it. A flash of white in a sea of whipped-raw black skin drew my attention, and I grabbed Kara's arm, pointing. "Look, look there—it's your father."

Kara scooted closer to me along the branch. She held her breath as she studied the camp below us. "It is him. And I see Tumelo down there as well." Biting her lip, she whispered, "They've been whipped. Badly. My father's back is all torn up."

I clutched her hand, grinning. Relief made me feel dizzy. "But they're alive."

The laborers started unloading long metal tubes from the train cart. Each of the tubes was large enough that it took two men to carry it. Tumelo and Mr. Harving staggered under the weight of their burden. A mountainous overseer wearing a white shirt splashed with blood and black mud cracked his whip against Tumelo's thigh. My cousin's eyes closed in momentary anguish.

"Those tubes… they kind of look like cannons, but they have no supports, and they're too small," Kara said, fiddling with dials on her binoculars for a better look. I nodded, not wanting to admit that I had no idea what a cannon was or how a metal tube big enough that two men struggled to lift it might be too small as a weapon.

Digging my fingers into the bark, I carefully adjusted my position on the branch so I could follow where Tumelo and Mr. Harving deposited their tube. They sank up to their calves in slick, green-tinged mud. The overseer walked behind them, sneering as he brought the lash down on Mr. Harving's pale flesh. A sensation like ants moved up my back as I imagined the snap and penetrating sting of it. I winced—when General Zuberi arrived, we would learn exactly what it felt like.

The two men hoisted the tube onto a black cart, alongside three others. Licks of painted fire covered the cart's matte sides. The tube fitted neatly into a slot. The space seemed to anchor it in place, but the end was open, allowing the tube to protrude beyond the cart's edge. Another overseer fed a string through a hole in the top of the "cannon." Arusei sat in the driver's seat, alongside one of his men. His lackey held the black leather reins, stretching down through the D rings of an enormous fitted harness to the tender mouth of a unicorn stallion.

Tumelo staggered back from the cart. He looked weary enough to drop to his knees in the mud and sleep in the filth. The overseer drove him away, but I kept my binoculars locked on Arusei.

His driver snapped the reins and the unicorn trudged forward. Another snap and the poor beast stumbled into a canter, dragging hundreds of pounds behind him. I watched as the driver maneuvered the unicorn through the tents, gathering speed as they went. A single horse could never have dragged a cart that heavy alone. A tandem team couldn't navigate with so much agility. An elephant would be too slow, too clumsy. Cold sweat trickled down my neck. They were like the carts of legends, but the unicorns themselves were not. Our stories talked of war-hungry beasts who sought out the enemy for their masters, fueled by bloodlust. The unicorn that dragged Arusei's cart now looked afraid and tired.

As soon as they were clear of the camps, Arusei reached down by his feet and lifted a thick slab of beechwood. He lit it as casually as Tumelo would strike a cigar and swiped the flaming stick across the tubes.

The bang that resulted was so loud I could hear it from the trees. Birds scattered around us. Smoke flew out of the ends of the tubes. Molten metal clung to the ground like silver frost around the cart. Arusei's secret weapons from Echalend had arrived.

"Does General Zuberi have those?" Kara asked. Her voice trembled.

"I've never seen anything like them," I whispered.

"Me either. I didn't even know we had them in Echalend."

The General's forces would have better rifles than my father's warriors. A few might carry gas that stung the eyes and poisoned the lungs. But they had nothing like that death cart. When my father and the General arrived, their forces would be entombed in metal by these portable volcanoes. General Zuberi's musings rang in my ears. He'd wondered why Arusei needed the unicorns so badly. Now we knew, but we'd have no chance to warn them.

Below us, Arusei's men stacked cart after cart with the tubes. Others brought metal plates and starting fitting them to the unicorns' bodies. Armor. They wanted to make it hard for the General's men to shoot the unicorns. When the men finished loading the carts, I noticed that they had six carts with tubes but no unicorns to pull them. It was a small comfort, knowing that by stealing the moonstone, we'd robbed them of their ability to field six of the death carts. I slipped my hand inside my shirt, assuring myself that it remained with me. The stone's glassy surface was warm with the heat radiating from my skin.

"We have to do something."

"What we can do? We won't have time to ride all the way back to the city. And we might miss them depending on the route they take. There is nothing we can do. We can't fight Arusei alone." I felt completely powerless to stop the carnage that would follow. The General would lose. My cousin would remain the slave of a crazed warlord forever. And all of Nazwimbe would fall.

"Set the unicorns free."

Her answer was so simple, so confident, that I wanted to believe we could do it. But the camp was armed, the overseers wary, and there was no way we could pass as emissaries again.

Kara gripped my arm. Leaves and needles from the tree clung to strands of her hair and that worrying sparkle of mischievous insanity glittered in her eyes again. "I have an idea."

Chapter Twelve

USING A piece of charcoal from our dwindling fire, I outlined Kara's eyes in smooth black. Then brushing white and gray ash across her lids, I blended the colors together into a smoky haze. Brilliant blue twinkled against the sultry darkness. Kara pinched her cheeks to bring on a wanton flush, as I raked my fingers through her hair to mess it up.

A mix of fear and longing spread through me. I wanted to drag her to my lips by her hair and use my body to stop her from doing this mad thing.

"Go on," she breathed. Her body trembled. "Mess me up. I need to look disheveled."

"Kara," I whispered, biting my lip and looking skyward so I wouldn't have to look into her eyes. "You don't have to do this. We can find another way to get into the camp."

"We've been through this already. I can't think of any other way."

"You could get hurt; you could end up like me...." My arms wrapped around my body, as I tried to squeeze out the hollowness inside my chest.

"We'll stick to the plan. Nothing will happen to me. I trust you."

I swallowed. The weight of the responsibility she was giving me settled so heavily in my stomach, it felt as though my insides had turned to molten lead. At the same time, a tingling lightness spread through my limbs as I struggled to draw breath. How could she ask me to do this? And why didn't I have another answer?

"We have to go now. If we don't, I'll start to chicken out, and I can't be the one who does that this time." She laid her hand on my back. "I'll be fine. I know you'll stop it soon enough."

Leaving the horses behind with the fire for protection until Bi Trembla's kitchen boy came to get them, we made our way across the grasslands separating us from Arusei's camp. In the foggy haze of the smoky night, all I could see were the outlines of tents, cast in shadows by his men's fires.

We crouched behind a termite mound, and I whipped out my binoculars. We peered into the darkness like a pair of hyena, waiting to ambush our target. Months of tracking elusive creatures served me well. I knew how to follow the line of shadow and stay camouflaged by the darkness. And I knew how to be patient. We would wait until we found the specific creature we were after.

The target stood against the stable block, back turned away from the camp. His knees were bent, and he pissed against the wall, groaning with relief as steam rose from the ground. I wrinkled my nose in revulsion, motioning Kara forward.

We dropped to our stomachs and began to crawl through the tall grass. I prayed that a leopard or a lioness didn't lay waiting for us behind a rock or concealed by a dip in the land. My heart felt frozen in my chest, and I struggled to keep my breathing even and quiet. Grass and termites clung to my skin, raising itching bumps across my forearms.

The repugnant prey buttoned his pants and leaned back against the wall, eyes half-closed. We crawled until we were twenty feet from him, hiding behind a pile of discarded meat bones and flour sacks. Then Kara slowly got to her feet.

Watching her go, my stomach churned with nerves. What had seemed like a decent plan before now seemed reckless. What if she couldn't pull this off? Worse still, what if he really hurt her, and I was too late to stop it? If something happened to her while I watched, I wasn't sure I could ever forgive myself.

"Hello?" she called softly into the darkness.

The man's eyes snapped open, and he licked his lips. I could almost see a line of drool coming out of gaping mouth. He edged over to Kara, slithering toward her like a grootslang on the hunt.

"I'm lost," she whimpered, spewing out the few words of our language she had memorized. Her tongue tripped on the Nazwim, making her seem all the more vulnerable. "When we ran from here, my guide left me."

His greedy eyes swept over her dirt-covered body and messy hair, taking in the smudges on her cheeks. A hand darted to her breast, the other squeezing the place between her legs so hard that she yelped. He didn't see the careful outlining of her eyes or notice the way Kara moved with him like a dancer after he released her, circling around so that his back was facing toward me.

"All alone, lovely girl," he said, leering and pressing his body close to hers. "No one to protect you. No fake chief to swat my hands away. If I help you, what will you give me in return?"

Listening to him made me sick. In that moment I hated both him and myself. I had allowed this, agreed to this insane proposal.

I knew Kara wouldn't understand what he was saying, but she understood the way he covered her mouth, dirty fingers pawing at the buttons of her shirt. Her pupils dilated in fear, but she didn't resist him as he pushed her to the ground, determined to see her plan through to the end. I swung my rifle over my shoulder and snuck toward him, a step at a time, hot bile rising in my throat. I wanted to shoot him, to hear the crack of his skull as metal burst through brain and popped out through his repulsive eye socket, but a gunshot would have alerted the whole camp. Everything inside me bubbled with anger. Year-old flashbacks juggled through my mind's eyes, unwanted. I felt the ground beneath my back, the fingers clawing at my neck and face, the deep burn of his blades…. How had I agreed to this?

I shook my head. If I didn't focus now, Kara might suffer the same fate.

If he saw me and screamed, the plan would be over. But his lust dulled his senses. He was too fixated on Kara to see my shadow as it fell over them. He didn't hear the soft crunch of the dry grass under my bare feet. I lunged, swinging my rifle as hard as I could. The butt collided with his temple. He slumped on top of Kara. She exhaled, tears of relief falling down her cheeks. I pushed him off her with my foot.

As he rolled to the side, rage coursed through me. How dare he? Never mind that this had been her plan all along, at that moment, I wished it had failed. I brought my rifle butt down again and again, hitting his stomach, his thighs, and his arms. Even after his body stilled, I couldn't stop. My arms felt disconnected from my body, operating on their own. I wanted to stop, but I wasn't in control anymore.

Shaking, Kara climbed to her feet. She wrapped her arms around my back and pressed my arms to my chest. Slowly, she pulled me back, away from her attacker. We embraced silently for a moment, listening to our breath slow. I looked down at the bleeding, unconscious man at my feet and let the anger flood out.

A quick glance around the stable block showed how lucky we'd been. He was the only guard watching the stables while the camp slumbered. Arusei imagined the unicorns safely locked away inside their iron stalls.

The air inside the stable was as stale and pungent as I remembered. The beautiful unicorns stood knee deep in dirty straw, listless with exhaustion. I put my hand through the bars of the first stallion's grate, trying to coax him to me. The animal didn't even look up.

Kara walked over to me and sighed. "It's going to be hard to get them to run. They have no energy left."

Suddenly, the stallion's ears perked up. He sniffed the air, staring at Kara with interest. He put his head over the half door of his stable, nuzzling her shoulders and chest. After he had made a thorough examination of her body, his head cocked in confusion, unable to find the source of the smell that had brought him to life.

The foal. Realization hit me as the stallion nibbled Kara's shoulder. She had carried the baby for days, and the stallion could smell his own kind on her. I wondered if something about the scent told him the baby hadn't been mutilated—he still had his precious horn and spirit. Kara scratched his forehead, her fingers lingering on the stub of his horn. I peered closer. I could see that the horn was growing. A single, light silver ring twisted around a tiny point.

Kara moved from stall to stall, letting the animals take in her scent. One by one the unicorns perked up. Rows of pricked ears stared back at us, waiting. I began pulling the bolts on their stable doors as fast I could.

At first the creatures just stared at the open doors. Some stood with dirty hay dripping out of their mouths, ears flickering back and forth. I pressed myself against the wall of the stable and held my breath. Then they poured out into the night, in a white river of long manes and sinewy muscle. Their hoofbeats fell softer than a cat's paw, ghosts.

Kara took my hand and pulled me toward the door. "We have to get out of here. We'll hide out until we see your father and the General's men. If we go back to camp, we might miss them. Hopefully they'll come tomorrow."

The last unicorn turned to face us at the doorway. The biggest of them all, the top of his back reached higher than my father's head. He let out a scream; a shrill melody floated on the air, rising higher like the climax of a song. Bending the muscular crest of his neck, the stallion touched his muzzle to his knees. And I could have sworn he was taking a bow.

THORNS PRESSED into my back and the bush's sulfurous odor made me sneeze. But if I rolled over, I'd have to move my head off the pillow of Kara's chest, so I sniffled and tried to ignore the pain. She curled closer to me in sleep, her hands entwined in the fabric of my shirt. A light layer of morning frost covered the ground around us. I shivered, pulling myself even closer to Kara to absorb her warmth. The bush's terrible scent kept predators away, so we didn't need a fire for protection, but I missed the heat. I didn't dare try to make one now, in case Arusei's men saw the smoke. It was a no-win choice between sleep inside the bush's prickly curtains or risk being eaten by predators.

Hoofbeats approached, and through the gaps in the leaves, I could make out a sturdy, shiny pair of black hooves. I held my breath and kept my body absolutely still.

"How could you let them get away?" a man's voice demanded. "You had one job. Only one."

"I never expected a chief's daughter to flee like some kind of wild animal in the middle of the night," another voice hissed back. "The foreigner, maybe. Who knows? Echalenders are a strange people."

How did they know I was a chief's daughter? I swallowed, wondering what they had done to Tumelo before putting him to work in order to get information about me. Did they know about Bi Trembla and the camp too?

The horse pulled at his reins, sniffing the grass below with interest. Its pink muzzle nosed the grass a foot away from my feet.

"Still," the first voice began. "Foreigner or not—stealing the General's goddaughter's pony? Poor Ariana was sick with worry. Up all night. And she's such a sweet child. Serves his brat of a grandson right, though."

"Too right," the second man chuckled. "Little wretch needs to learn to share his toys. I can't believe they jumped over the wall on those things. That takes guts."

I sucked in a deep breath. These men weren't from Arusei at all. Even if he had tortured Tumelo until my cousin broke, Tumelo could not have revealed our midnight pony heist. I sat up, scratching my arms on brambles and thorns and crawled out of the bush.

The horse's head snapped up, and he shied sideways, nearly dumping one of his riders. He was an enormous draft animal, with hooves the size of plates and a deep, powerful chest. The second rider jumped down as soon as he saw me. He looked me up and down, eyes jumping to the yellow dusting of pollen that covered my hair.

"My God," he exclaimed, and then rolled his eyes. "Ran away, rode all this way, just to lie sleeping in a bush? We had bushes in Mugdani, you know. If you wanted one instead of a bed, you could have saved yourself all this trouble and asked."

He grasped my arm, as if afraid I might crawl back under the foliage and disappear again before he could bring me to his boss.

I snatched my arm away. He was one of the General's close attendants. I recognized him from the day before. "You're early. We didn't expect you until this afternoon or maybe tomorrow."

"And you're in a world of trouble," he said, exchanging glances with his companion. "Your father was beside himself. So yes, we ended up coming as soon as we could."

Kara climbed out of the bush to stand behind me, rubbing her eyes. Ant bites and thorn scratches covered both of her arms. I winced for her as she attacked the red bumps with her nails. Her hair looked like a living creature: ants moved across the red strands, leaves and berries clung to the knotted nest.

"Where is the rest of the army?" she asked, putting her head between her legs and combing her hair with her fingers to shake out the ants.

"We're just scouts, sent to look for you. They're just over the ridge, setting up camp. We left before dawn," the second rider grumbled. He lifted his foot to the horse's stirrup to climb up, but his companion shook his head.

"We should let them ride."

"Let them ride after all the problems they've caused?" the attendant asked, chuckling and rubbing the back of his head. "You have to be kidding."

The other rider swung off the horse, shaking his head. "The General will not be pleased if we make two women walk while we ride, especially a chief's daughter." He held the stirrup and motioned for Kara to mount. "Any trouble they've caused isn't for us to deal with. We take them to General Zuberi and Chief Adebayo. Then it's their problem."

"It's still not fair," the first attendant whined. "We've been up for hours."

"And they slept in a bush covered in ants. Do you really want to compare worst nights? Besides, if they're on the horse and we're holding the reins, they can't run away again."

I swallowed. Suddenly, I wished the General had ignored my father and chosen to sleep in. Father alone was formidable enough when truly angry, but the General had a terrifying reputation. We might have been safer with Arusei.

WHEN WE reached the edge of the General's camp, I understood why Zuberi had wanted so much time to prepare. The camp spanned acres, built along a perfect grid. Identical rows of blue and black soldiers' tents framed a central square. It looked almost as if someone had patrolled with a ruler, perfectly aligning the camp like an enormous architectural drawing.

Stacks of weapons lay outside each tent: pile after pile of rifles, poison bombs, and claw-blades. I almost smirked. Without Arusei's death carts, the General's men could overrun the poachers with ease. As we approached the central square, the attendants brought the horse to a halt outside the largest tent. I pressed my lips together to vanish the smile. Better to look contrite.

We dismounted, and the attendant rushed inside to announce us. Seconds later the General appeared through the tent flap. His dark eyes stormed, and he tapped his cane on the ground. He jabbed his finger at me. "Just her. The foreigner can stay outside."

The ferocity in his eyes made my legs shake. We hadn't eaten in over twenty hours, but fear made my bowels churn. This was it. It probably wouldn't even matter what I told him about the unicorns. I bowed my head and followed him into the tent.

Inside, the General lowered himself into a leather chair at one end of a long table. Twelve unoccupied wood chairs sat around it, so I tentatively pulled out the one farthest away from him and perched on the edge. Attendants scurried around the tent, hanging drapes and mosquito nets. General Zuberi cleared his throat, and the servants stopped immediately and filed out of the tent in a line. I shuddered, feeling much exposed now that we were alone. Any man who could order people about by clearing phlegm from his throat needed to be feared.

General Zuberi steepled his fingers. "You disobeyed an express command, from both myself and your father."

I squirmed in my chair. "I know."

"I should have both of you publicly horsewhipped for your insolence."

I looked down and ran my finger over the cracks in the table, hardly daring to breathe. He'd said *should*, which meant he still might decide not to. Or at least allow me to save Kara.

"Do you want to explain to me why you disobeyed me? With the foreigner, I understand. She is not accustomed to our ways. Plus, the man imprisoned is her father. Doesn't know our history or our laws. She has no reason to trust my reputation. But you are a chief's daughter. I expected much better."

"We just had to know. We couldn't sit and do nothing. We had to know if they were alive." I took a deep breath. It was tempting to look down at my feet and answer his questions in monosyllables. But the General wouldn't respect me for that. "But, sir—it's a good thing we did. Last night we snuck into Arusei's camp."

"You did what?" the General hissed. Then he banged his fist on the table. "This is exactly why your father was so insistent we leave immediately. He knew you would do something rash and stupid—"

Against all sense of self-preservation, I cut him off. Words flew out. I needed him to know everything, before I lost the nerve. "But sir—Arusei's weapons from Echalend… they arrived. We saw them unload the train. He has these tubes…. Kara called them cannons… but he lines them up on carts and uses the unicorns to pull them. We set the unicorns free. If we hadn't, many of your men would have died."

The General went very quiet, staring at me across the table. He licked his lips, and when he finally spoke, I heard the smallest note of uncertainty in his iron voice. "He had cannons?"

I nodded. "Mobile cannons. They were like death carts. Each unicorn could pull four at once. Fast."

General Zuberi took a deep, jagged breath. His eyes scanned my face. "That's what he needed them for. You freed them all?"

"Yes, and before when we snuck in, we stole his moonstone—that's how he attracts them. He can't replace them. At least not until he finds another stone."

He stroked his chin and drummed his fingers on the table again as he thought. "Then we must act before he has chance to do so. He will still be able to load those cannons, but without something to pull them, they will be difficult to move into place. If we can ambush them from the sides of his camp, they will have no chance to use them. I have brought three hundred armed men with me. We will arrest them within minutes."

He rose slowly from his chair, legs shaking without his cane. I felt the urge to go and offer him my arm, but I doubted he would appreciate any acknowledgment of his weakness. "I can't condone your disobedience outside this tent. You will understand that appearances have to be upheld. But let us say, between you and I, that I am not displeased."

Limping, he came toward me and laid his hand on my shoulder. "Those cannons would have ripped our men to shreds. I don't know how you girls did it, but doing so was very brave. My warriors are also brave, but sometimes I wish I had more like you around me, with the courage to follow themselves."

I looked down at my hands. "Thank you, sir."

"Your cousin and the girl's father… they are alive, yes?"

"Yes, Arusei enslaved them. Please… when you arrest Arusei, most of the laborers have been forced. They don't want to work for him. Don't shoot them."

He shook his head in disgust. "Arusei is a monster. Even when he was a child, we knew what he would grow up to become. He and those who served him willingly will be condemned to the Pits. The others we will restore to their families."

I closed my eyes, thanking the gods I never prayed to that Tumelo would soon be home.

General Zuberi turned toward the tent flap. "I will instruct the attendants to find you and the foreign girl a tent, food, and a hot bath."

"Kara and I have guns—"

The General raised his hand, scowling. "You're not a trained warrior, and the presence of women will distract the men on the field. In this you will obey me."

I walked behind him, so that we were at eye level. "I'm a good fighter, just because I'm a woman—"

His cane snaked out and whacked my calves so hard I nearly screamed.

"You forget yourself," the General said. "I like you. I like your ideas. But I have explained to you why your disobedience could jeopardize our mission. I won't have a young girl's silly ideas about becoming some sort of warrior princess cost any of my men's lives. You're a good tracker, and you have a good brain. Stick to your talents. If I find you at Arusei's camp during our attack, I will have you horsewhipped. No matter the outcome."

I hung my head as the General walked out of the tent, slinking away without looking at him again.

Chapter Thirteen

FED, BATHED, and warm, we wrapped ourselves in a thick blanket and floated in the airy comfort of the feather mattress until evening. I woke with my arm slung over Kara's back, to the sounds of men marching. I wanted to stay and admire the contrast between our skin and the graceful arch of her sleeping back, but despite what the General had threatened, I couldn't imagine staying in bed while his army attacked Arusei's camp. Zuberi and his men would be focused on the poachers, and my father would play the part he was given—someone had to make sure Tumelo and Mr. Harving made it to safety.

With a small sigh, I slid out from under the white, velvet blanket. When had I become such a daredevil? Kara mumbled in her sleep. I pulled on my clothes, hesitating to look at her before I slipped out the door. When Kara woke up, she'd kill me for leaving her behind like this. We were a team, but she was safe here, away from the battle like General Zuberi had ordered. Besides, I was already scarred and a few whip marks wouldn't make my body any uglier. But for Kara, I wondered what they would mean when she returned to Echalend.

I squeezed my eyes shut and rushed out the door to stop the flow of emotion. I couldn't think about her return right now.

Slipping unnoticed among the soldiers as they saddled their horses and loaded equipment into wagons, I crept to the makeshift stables to find Elikia. Most of the horses were already out of their stalls and the attendants took no notice of me as I peered over doors, swiping a spare bridle as I went.

Elikia munched hay in a stall at the very end of the block. When she saw me, her head lifted and she nickered softly, ears twitching back and forth. I reached in to scratch her forehead, and she leaned into my touch. "I'm sorry I left you behind, girl."

My fingers curled around the metal bolt and I tried to tug it open. It held fast. Looking down, I groaned. A large silver padlock dangled from the bolt, securing it place. General Zuberi had anticipated that I might not obey him and had taken extra precautions. Scanning the stalls of the other remaining horses, I realized that all of them were locked as well. Damn it.

"Ahem."

Closing my eyes, I slowly turned around. Kara stood with her arms crossed over her chest, wearing the silken nightgown the general's attendants had put aside for her. Her long white legs were bare, but she had hastily stuffed her feet into a pair of sturdy leather boots. Smudged circles of the coal she'd only half washed off made her eyes look even fiercer than usual. Her wild hair had been pinned back into a quick ponytail.

"Please don't tell me you were thinking of doing something stupid without me."

"I—"

She scowled. "That was rhetorical. And don't lie to me either. At least I caught you before you left."

I pointed to the lock on Elikia's stall door. "We're not going anywhere."

Kara rolled her eyes, flashing me a devious grin. She pulled a pin out of her hair and knelt by the lock. "You have no imagination, sometimes."

"I suppose you just picked that up at boarding school as well."

She smirked as the lock clicked open and then tucked the pin back into her red curls. "Political rallies, remember? My father wasn't totally naïve. He did try to keep me from going sometimes."

Looking around to make sure none of the attendants were watching us, I rushed inside the stall, throwing the reins over

Elikia's head and hopping aboard while Kara picked the lock on Brekna's stall. The stallion was fresh, and when she swung onto his back he burst from his stable, prancing about and snorting. I reached over and gave one of his reins a sharp jerk, hoping he would get the message and start behaving.

Most of the camp had gone dark, as the army had taken their torches with them on the march. I didn't want to light a torch of our own until after we made it out of the camp, so we had to rely on the moon and on the horses' keener eyesight to navigate through the maze of pitched tents.

While the army left the camp from the west, I took us east. We worked our way through the grasslands in a wide arch before falling into place a few hundred meters behind the General's slowest supply carts. Over the clamor of wheels, groaning oxen, marching feet, and a hundred war stallions, nobody noticed us trailing behind them, bathed in shadow. I didn't understand how the General could possibly believe he'd have the advantage of surprise, with all the noise his troops made. At least they would frighten away any predators hiding in the long grass.

When the warm haze of Arusei's camp became visible over the hill, I motioned to Kara, and we slipped away, urging our horses back into the little oasis to hide. The General's drummers began to beat the huge barrels, carried between two elephants at the start of the column. The sun slowly crept up behind the poacher's camp, illuminating the muddy labyrinth in a bath of red light. I shuddered. The way the rays reflected off the pools of dirty water made it look like blood ran through the site already.

A loud bang returned the grim overture of the General's drums. My breath stopped, my throat closing with fear. That was a cannon shot. Molten metal punched a hole in the middle of the column, raining burning death over a dozen men before they even had time to scream.

"Go!" General Zuberi yelled above the chaos. "We can't give them time to reload."

His men began pouring into the camp. As I predicted, none of Arusei's slaves fought, but the poachers used their army of laborers as camouflage. They hid amongst them, concealing their guns. The General's men looked around in confusion for the enemy, unable to distinguish between the poachers and their kidnapped victims. A shot rang out, and one of the drummers tumbled down from the elephant.

"Arrest all of them!" General Zuberi screamed, kicking his white horse forward into the melee. "We will sort through them once we have them in chains."

A collective war howl erupted from the General's men, and they set upon the poachers. More shots fired, and I saw drops of blood fly as the claw-blades the warriors wore ripped through flesh.

I swallowed, turning away. The slash of those claws triggered unwanted memories. Movement at the edge of the trees caught my eye, and I heard the crunch of dry grass. Turning Elikia to face the source of the sound, I pulled out my binoculars and focused in.

At first all I could see was the smooth black of horsehair peeking through the leaves. I adjusted the dials and scanned upward, looking for the man's face. I gazed into his dark eyes, glittering with spite. *Arusei.*

While his men fought to avoid the Pits, their leader snuck away through the quiet fields, trying to melt into the dim light of the early morning. The cowardice of it made me hate Arusei even more. And if we'd stayed at the camp, like the General ordered, nobody would have seen him sneak away. With all the powerful contacts he had made abroad, I was sure he could find allies willing to help him out of the country.

There was no way I would let him escape. He'd kidnapped my cousin, tortured the only family member who had always had my back. I pulled my rifle over my shoulder and took aim.

"What is it? What are you doing?" Kara whispered.

Swallowing hard, my fingers trembling, I pulled the trigger.

The rifle kicked back with enough force to leave my shoulder numb.

"Son a bitch!" Arusei screamed as the bullet lodged in his shinbone. His horse squealed, spinning around on its haunches. Arusei dropped from the saddle like a sack of corn, clutching his leg and howling.

"You shot him. I can't believe you actually shot him." Kara covered her mouth.

"He'll live," I said, nudging Elikia forward out of the trees. I pulled my shawl over my head, covering my face so he couldn't recognize me, leaving Kara behind in the woods. Blood pounded in my ears, and my hands shook so much that I struggled to hold my reins. Part of me couldn't believe I'd shot him either.

As I drew my horse alongside him, Arusei looked up. His howls had quieted to pain-filled moans and whimpers as he struggled to bind the wound with strips of cloth torn from his jacket.

"Going to finish the job?" He glared at me, eyes steady and unafraid.

I shook my head, pushing him over onto his back with my foot. "I'll leave it up to you. Scream loud enough, and I'm sure the General's forces will pick you up. Or you could let an animal finish you off—but sometimes they start with the feet."

His eyes widened in real fear now. I turned Elikia around and motioned for Kara. We needed to get back to camp or risk being caught. The General's soldiers would have heard the shot and someone would already be on their way to investigate now, whether Arusei screamed or not. But he didn't know that. And while I could never be cruel enough to leave someone—even a man like Arusei—to a death by wild animals, I could let him think that I would.

"We're actually going to leave him?" Kara hissed.

I nodded, and for once, she didn't argue.

I PEERED out from our tent flap. We'd snuck back into camp without being noticed, and Kara had curled back into an exhausted ball beneath the duvet. The clatter of metal and groaning, tired horses had roused me from the bed.

General Zuberi rode at the head of a large column. The warriors at the front of the column dragged men in chains behind them. The prisoners wore muzzles with metal bars over their tongues and thick shackles connected their limbs. A few of them cried openly, wailing around the gags, knowing they were destined for the Pits. A team of horses dragged Arusei's own gilded cage along behind them. Inside, a crumbled figure sat huddled and naked in the corner with his head in his hands. Some of the younger soldiers threw things at him through the bars. An apple core hit his face and Arusei shrank away, covering his eyes. Spotting my father, I rushed out to greet him.

Father raised his eyebrows when he saw me, but from the proud twinkle in his eye and the way he bit his lip, I could tell that the General had told him of the conversation in the tent.

He hugged me with one arm, kissing the top of my head. "Glad to find you here and see you have some sense after all."

I stuck my tongue out at him, almost sighing with relief that none of the attendants had reported us.

Father's gaze traveled back to Arusei's cage and a cruel gleam appeared in his eyes. "He won't last long in the Pits. I bet he'll take the way out the first time the dagger is offered. But General Zuberi is thinking about making special provisions, just for him. Five year gaps between offerings."

I shuddered. A minimum sentence of five years in the Pits, without death as a means of escape. Even Arusei might not deserve that.

"Mnemba." I heard Tumelo's voice, and I whirled around, scanning the rows of warriors.

He stepped forward, covered in a coarse brown blanket. I dove for him, wrapping my arms around him tighter than a constricting python. He winced, squeezing me back with his free arm. The column of warriors streamed past us. "Not so hard. I have lots of whip marks on my back."

144

Grudgingly, I loosened my hold on him. In just a few days, he looked and felt smaller. His cheeks had a strange pinched look to them. Dark bags hung under his eyes. But the biggest difference was how he carried himself. My cousin always walked proudly, with his chest out, daring the world. Now his back was hunched and his chest caved in.

"Are you okay?" I asked. Rethinking, "Will you be okay?"

Tumelo ran a hand over my head, messing up my new braids. "I'll be fine. The real question is—did you bring my cigars?"

I groaned. Cigars—of all the things he could want right now: a bed, some food, a glass of clean water... he wanted his dragon's breath sticks. "Don't you think you should eat something first?"

Tumelo pressed his lips together, shaking his head. "The breath of life, Mnemba! After all I've been through, how could you deny it to me?"

Rolling my eyes, I patted his shoulder. "Mama keeps saying you're killing yourself from the inside out, but I'm sure if you ask him nicely, Father will have one stashed away somewhere."

"How is your blessed mama? I heard you finally went home. I should get myself kidnapped and enslaved more often."

At least his time under Arusei's yoke had done nothing to damage his spirit or his sense of humor. I resisted the urge to slap him, for the sake of his broken body. Looking past him, I asked, "Where is Kara's father?"

"Medic's tent."

I stared at him with disbelief, my heart pounding. How could something have happened to him now, right before he was rescued? And how could I possibly tell Kara? "Was he shot? What happened?"

Tumelo shook his head. "No, no. Nothing like that. But his back's infected, and he needs some stitches. They've lined all the ones up needing medical attention. He'll probably be there half the night. You might as well rest in your tent. I'll tell him where to find you. They've got us sharing."

I let myself exhale. "Thank goodness, I couldn't have told Kara—"

"How is your saucy redhead? Traumatized? Is she even sexier as the damsel in distress?"

Whip sores be damned, I punched his shoulder.

"Not denying it anymore, hmm?" He smirked. Turning me around, he gave me a push. "Well go on, then. Unless you're going to be useful and track down a cigar for me, get back to your ladylove. I'll tell her father where to find you in a few hours when the medics set him free."

KARA STILL slept curled in a fetal position, her arm reaching over her back into the space I'd vacated. I crawled back into the comfort of our bed. *Our*. Calling it that made a dizzy warmth spread through my body. I lifted her arm and melted back into my position, whispering against her neck. "Your father's back."

Her eyes fluttered open. "What, have you seen him? Where is he?"

"He's getting a few stitches. Nothing major. Tumelo said he'd send him to find you later. It's going to be a while—apparently there's a line."

"He's safe. That's what matters." She closed her eyes as she nestled into my chest. Warm feet pressed against my freezing legs. "I didn't even feel you get up. How's Tumelo?"

"A little battered but still making fun of me, so he can't be too bad." I paused, picking at the sheets as I muttered, "He knows about us."

Kara propped herself up on one elbow and looked into my eyes. For a moment I mistook the intensity in her stare for accusation. I kicked myself for being so careless—for letting Tumelo suspect. She was leaving in less than a week to go home. And she had a life there. Things, a fancy house, a fiancé, her research. How could she be happy here? In a backward, unfamiliar country, where she didn't speak the language? The warmth of the blankets suddenly

146

felt overwhelming. I shoved the sheets aside and let the cold night air sting my legs.

"I don't care." She reached for my hand, and my fingers froze in her grasp. "I love you, and whatever my father says, I'm not going back."

"What?" I croaked. I fought for words, and my mind came up blank.

Kara sighed, slapping my hand playfully. "You're not supposed to say 'what' when someone tells you they love you."

"How?" I whispered. Fear and bile rose in my throat. I couldn't relish the moment, not yet. I needed her to say it again. "Don't say you're going to stay here when we both know it's impossible."

"Despite everything that has happened, I have never felt more alive than I have in the last week. I don't want to go back to my books and my big house. We look after each other. We're a team. If I stay here, my father can say I've gone mad or something. The king won't press it, not if I don't return." She sucked in a deep breath. "No one has ever looked at me like you do. At home, most people think I'm too fat."

"How do I look at you?"

"Like you want to protect me and devour me whole at the same time."

Finally, I let what she was saying sink in. She loved me. She wasn't leaving. I was more than an adventure. I exhaled, lowered my mouth to the skin of her thigh, nibbling the dimpled flesh. "I love you too."

Her fingers ran along the ridges between my cornrows. Tossing the blanket over my back, she sat up, raising the covers like a tent over our heads. Firelight glowed through the white, and I felt like we were encased in a sunlit cloud. Kara's fingers worked their way down to my shoulders and then lower, to my chest, cupping my dark breasts in her pale hands.

When I pressed my mouth to hers, relief flooded through my body. I felt no trace of fear. Our kiss was messy. My tongue lapped against hers like a dying man catching rain. The desperate pressure of her lips against mine hurt. My lips were too dry. Hers too wet. Still, in the passionate wrongness of it, I found perfection.

"Ahem," said a male voice on the outside of our fortress.

With shaking fingers, Kara lowered the cover.

Tumelo stood looking down at us, his eyes laughing. But a step behind him, bearing no trace of a smile whatsoever, was Mr. Harving.

Tumelo had lied twice. Mr. Harving stumbled forward, using a crutch to support his weight. Whatever injury he'd suffered was a lot worse than a few stitches, and the medic had prioritized him. Kara and I sprang apart; the action sealed our guilt.

"Kara?" Mr. Harving asked, hovering at the edge of the bed. "What is going on? What are you doing?"

Over his head, Tumelo mouthed, "Sorry!"

If the situation hadn't been so serious, I would have thrown my socks at him.

Kara sat up slowly, lifting her chin to meet her father's eye. "I'm in love with her."

Despite what he had just caught us doing, Mr. Harving's eyes bulged in shock. "Don't be ridiculous, Kara. You've known her less than two weeks. We're leaving in a few days and if you ask me, the sooner we get out of this hellish place and away from poachers, the better."

"I'm in love with her," Kara repeated, and my eyes welled with tears. No amount of lip biting could stop the flow of emotion now. "I'm not going back with you. I hope you'll visit me, and you can tell people whatever you like: that I got sick, that your capture drove me mad and I've been institutionalized, the truth. But I'm not going back."

"What about Timothy?"

Kara shrugged. "What about him? We don't care for each other. If I stay here, the king will declare me as good as dead. The astrologer will find someone else for Timothy. Maybe he'll get lucky and find someone he's in love with as well."

"You don't know the first thing about love!" Mr. Harving shouted, wincing in pain as he stepped onto his bad leg. "Love grows over time. It's slow. It develops. What you feel is lust, driven by this whole accursed situation."

Kara's chin jutted stubbornly. "It's not."

"What will you do here? Live in a tent in the wilderness? You'll have no prospects. No job. What about our research?" Mr. Harving's voice broke. He fished a dirty handkerchief out of his pocket and blew his nose. "You honestly want me to leave you here, with nothing but your feelings? Feelings won't feed you, Kara. And in a month's time when you've realized you've made a mistake? You'll be disgraced. You'll come back to Echalend and none of our friends will see you. I can't do that. I care too much for you."

Tumelo stepped forward. "I'll give her a job."

"If you think I'm going to let my only child guide tourists alone in the Nazwimbe backcountry—"

"Not as a guide," Tumelo interrupted. He pulled a cigar out of his pocket and lit it with relish. "As an office manager. I want to expand our business. But I hate all the correspondence. Organizing with foreigners. She can do that."

Both Harvings stared at him. Kara's face broke into a wide smile while Mr. Harving looked about to spit in Tumelo's face. I longed to get up and hug him, for giving me hope yet again.

"My daughter is too well educated—"

"I'll take it." Kara beamed.

Mr. Harving took his daughter by the shoulders. He had tears openly dripping down his cheeks. "Sweetheart, I love you. I want you to be happy. But please, think about what you're doing. This love, lust… it's unnatural, it's unsanctioned. If it's real, then neither of those things matter to me. Your happiness comes first. But I don't want you to make a decision you'll come to regret."

"Look, you have two years to decide, right?" I asked, looking from father to daughter. "If it's lust, then it'll fade and we can have her back on a boat to you by the New Year. You're researchers.

She can continue the research here. Nobody at your home needs to know anything other than that, for now. If it's love, well, then she stays and all the social consequences of Echalend will never reach her here."

"I won't change my mind!" Kara stammered. "How can you think that, after what I just said?"

Tumelo blew a thick ring of smoke toward her, silencing her outburst by sending her into a coughing fit. He knew a bargain when he heard it.

Mr. Harving wiped tears from his eyes, thinking. "I want you to be happy. That's all I've ever wanted for you."

"I won't be happy with Timothy. You know that." Kara fanned Tumelo's smoke away and took a ragged breath. "I loved Mama, but she never made *you* truly happy, did she?"

Mr. Harving looked at his shoes. My heart beat so fast and hard I was sure he could hear it. After a long pause, he whispered, "You can stay."

Kara threw her arms around him and buried her face his chest. "I'll write to you every week."

Mr. Harving blew his nose into his handkerchief again and then ruffled his daughter's hair. "You have to promise me that you'll keep thinking about what I said. About returning."

Looking from me to Tumelo, Kara said, "Can you give us some time alone?"

I wanted to stay, to make sure Mr. Harving wouldn't take back his permission, but Tumelo grabbed me by the arm and marched me out of the tent before I could recover from the shock of it all. She was staying, for now; she was really staying.

WHILE KARA said good-bye to her father, I wandered the camp. Most of the warriors were too tired to notice me as I wound my way in and out of the tents. They reclined on their pallets, cleaning superficial cuts and tearing bites of jerky from slabs the length of their arms.

On the outskirts of the camp, Arusei's men sat chained to wooden posts. Their hands were bound behind their backs, chained to the top of the posts, stretching their arms back as they knelt. I picked my way through the prisoners to Arusei's gilded cage. He didn't move forward as I approached, so I pressed right up against the bars, peering through. He was tied against the back corner, his wrists bound to the bars. Someone had bandaged and cleaned the leg I'd shot. The General wouldn't give him the relative mercy of a quick death by blood-loss. His eyes followed me; his pupils were wide and his face held a dark mixture of loathing, respect, and amusement. A hasty rope gag passed through his lips. I glanced around. None of the other prisoners were gagged. It made me wonder what the General didn't want him to say.

Biting my lip, I looked around for guards. A few of them mulled about, lazily swinging their rifles and talking to one another.

I reached through the bars and unfastened the gag. Lightning fast, he sank his teeth into my arm. I gasped, fighting not to scream as I wrenched my arm back away from him.

"That was for the leg wound." He smirked.

I clutched my arm to my chest, and blood bubbled from the circular wound. Reaching through the bars again, I smacked his wounded shin, and this time it was him who bit back a scream.

Closing his eyes and choking, like he swallowed down vomit, he asked, "What is it you want to ask me?"

"What is it the General doesn't want me to ask you? Why were you gagged?"

He shrugged. "Maybe he thought I would shout obscenities at nice little girls like you. Or maybe not. Promise me you'll drive a dagger into my back after I tell you."

"I won't." After everything I had seen him do, I wouldn't let any amount of curiosity get in the way of justice.

Arusei laughed, flashing red, blood-covered teeth. "Worth a try."

"Why did you do any of this?" I asked. "The General says you wanted to take over Nazwimbe."

"He's right, but I bet he didn't tell you why."

"You're power hungry. My father said this isn't the first time you've tried this shit."

Firelight made the anger in his eyes glisten. "This strange utopia where no one is starving and we all exist without electricity or factories. It can't last. It's a fantasy. The world is changing around us, and Zuberi doesn't see it. His son will be the same. We have to modernize, or we'll be choked out."

"You kidnapped and enslaved people. You took my cousin prisoner. You can't just try to pretend you're some kind of modernizing savior," I spat. I remembered the stench of Arusei's camp, the whip sores on the bodies of his laborers. How could he think that kind of rule would be progress for Nazwimbe?

"Yes," he admitted, shrugging again. "I'm not saying I'm a good man, girl, but I would be good for this country."

"By turning people into slaves?"

"By turning a few people into slaves so that all of us don't end up that way."

I shook my head. "You're mad. Our neighbors don't want that. We've had peaceful relations with them for years."

"Peaceful in terms of the battlefield, yes. But they're draining us slowly on trade terms, and what can we do to stop them? You either keep up or you get dragged along behind in the dirt like an animal."

"What doesn't he want anybody to ask you?" My voice felt stuck in my throat, but I forced it up, nearly gagging on the words.

"About the moonstone. He doesn't want me to tell anyone that it actually works." His lips curled into another grotesque smile. "For him, peacekeeping is about suppression. If he keeps things the way they are, then everyone is satisfied that he's doing the right thing, even if the world moves on. Now that the stone is his, he'll use it to keep things the same. Have you ever seen a unicorn in battle frenzy? If you thought our carts were terrifying, imagine what they would be like pulled by a mad demon, with only blood on its mind. Soon, I expect we'll see our beloved General riding a unicorn stallion on his way to market. One of the men will tell how we tamed them, and that will be it."

"He won't do that." My mouth set in a firm line.

"You give him too much credit, little girl."

"He won't." Folding my arms across my chest again, I marched away from Arusei's gilded prison. I had no way of knowing whether he was lying to me or not. General Zuberi had been a fixture from long before I was born. My father revered him. But if there was any chance that he might use the moonstone to entrap the unicorns and create living weapons as Arusei had tried to do, I wouldn't let him have it. I wouldn't let anyone have it. Tumelo's little safari camp on the savanna was my home now and the elusive, mythical unicorns were a part of it. Before, I'd seen them as a challenge—the object of a game I played against myself and the other guides to forget bad memories. But they were part of Kara's soul, her first true love. And that meant they were part of me now too.

I crept out to Elikia's stable. In the lazy afterglow of the battle, no one asked any questions as I pulled my old saddlebags from the tack trunk. No one had thought to rummage through the old clothes, weathered boots, and safari equipment. My fingers brushed against the moonstone's cold, dead surface. A shiver went through my body. I would keep it, and everything I loved, safe.

A FEW weeks later, Kara and I rode through the thick brush, relishing the cool morning wind on our last day of freedom before a new tour group arrived—a strange couple who had written that they didn't eat meat or products made with corn flour. Bi Trembla was already raging. I hoped they were prepared to live on mangos and oatmeal for two weeks.

The unicorn foal trotted at Brekna's heels, skipping through the grass like a puppy, kicking at butterflies and sneezing as the wispy plants tickled his sensitive nose. Tumelo had named him *Moshi Nyeupe*—white smoke—after his favorite pastime. The name had stuck, in part because Tumelo flatly refused any other suggestions and because he had taught the baby his name by bribing him with bits of mango pulp. The little unicorn didn't respond when we called him anything else.

Moshi snapped playfully at Brekna's fetlocks and the big stallion stopped in his tracks, turning his head to glare at the youngster. The foal darted under his belly. I moved Elikia alongside the bewildered stallion and bent in my saddle to pick the tiny foal up. Although he had grown, he was still light enough to scoop up with one arm. He struggled in my hold as I settled him in front of my saddle, irritated at losing his newfound freedom. We passed a herd of impala, grazing calmly on the dew-covered grass. Moshi squirmed even harder, desperate to investigate creatures with horns like his own.

Kara chuckled and clicked to the pack mules trailing behind her. "He's going to be impossible once he gets too big to lift. Bi Trembla's right. We have to train him to lead on a rope."

"We have time." I stroked the foal's soft fur.

After dismounting by the riverbank, I took the saddlebags off the mules, pulling out the things I'd taken for the picnic and tucking the foal into the bags in their place. I spread a blanket out by the river's edge and laid out two baskets. Kara lay down on the blanket, her red hair falling softly around her shoulders. She closed her eyes, letting the early morning rays of sun dance across her face. I leaned over and brushed a kiss across her lips, then slid an oat biscuit between her teeth. Her eyes opened a crack, and she grinned.

"Sit up," I said, placing one of the baskets between us. "Look what I've brought."

She flipped the lid open and plunged her hand in, withdrawing it with a skeptical crinkle of her nose.

I reached in and pulled out a red hunk of raw meat. It squished and dripped between my fingers.

Kara covered her mouth. "I knew I should have packed breakfast instead of letting you do it. Do you need to build a fire so we can cook that?"

I shook my head, throwing the meat into the river. A moment later, a blonde head poked up from the surface. The mermaid smiled demurely and then dove for the meat. When she surfaced again, grinning, she had blood between her perfect, straight teeth.

"Give me some." Kara laughed. She pulled out an enormous handful of meat, breaking it into smaller chunks before tossing it into the water. Another mermaid streamed toward it from behind a rock, elbowing the blonde aside.

Reaching for Kara's free hand, I folded my fingers into hers. Together, we sat hand in hand, looking out across the shimmering water. We listened to the phoenixes sing, throwing chunks of goat meat into the crystal water, as the mermaids wrestled for blood.

The Beasts of Nazwimbe
A Definitive Guide by K.L. Harving

The Journal of the Strange and Exotic

J.R Root & Associates Publications: Echalend, 1892.

Introduction

The Republic of Nazwimbe is home to some of the world's most diverse, elusive, and dangerous creatures. Uniquely among Echalenders, I have now made my home in the savanna of Nazwimbe, documenting and studying these amazing creatures firsthand. I have concluded that our existing literature in Echalend draws largely from myth rather than fact. Through my own observation and by communicating with the people of Nazwimbe, who have lived among these striking creatures for centuries, I hope to right many of the misconceptions pervading popular scientific literature. At the time of going to press, the notes I have enclosed on the species are accurate to the extent of my knowledge. Further investigation and inquiry is necessary, and I hope to inspire more eminent researchers than myself to take an interest in the fauna of Nazwimbe.

Love from afar,
K.L. Harving

Classification

Abada—A two-horned subspecies of genus *Unicornalis*. Unlike its white cousin, the Abada dwells in herds of five to fifteen individuals and can often be observed grazing alongside the wildebeest and the common zebra—thus giving rise to the myth that the Abada resulted from the liaison of these two species. Shorter in stature than the White Unicorn, the Abada has a brown coat with stripes winding up its haunches. The Abada is a peaceful herbivore and can be easily approached.

Caladrius—A water-dwelling bird with long stork-like legs. Prized and often hunted for its turquoise, cerulean, and bright orange feathers, the Caladrius now hovers on the verge of extinction with fewer than three hundred mating pairs still living in Nazwimbe. Its feathers adorn the headdresses of chieftains throughout Nazwimbe, though efforts are being made to convince locals to use Phoenix or Nkombe feathers instead to preserve the dwindling population. It prefers to nest in shallow waters and feeds on small insects.

Chimera—A dangerous predator that feeds on elephants and hippos. The Chimera has a lionlike head with two horns, the body of a great cat and a second head on its tail, with the form of a snake. The Chimera should be approached with extreme caution and only when it has recently fed, and then only when accompanied by a guide or expert. This predator prefers to live in tree-covered areas, so that it can ambush its prey from above.

Grelbok—Unique among the animal kingdom, this small antelope can digest and process minerals, using the metals to build up its elaborate horns. The solid horns of the Grelbok grow throughout its lifetime, and never fall off. The Grelbok is a rare and elusive creature—seeing one in the wild is thought to bring a lifetime of luck.

Griffin—A close relative of the Chimera, the Griffin possesses the head and wings of an eagle and the body of a powerful cat. In Nazwimbe, two subspecies of Griffin exist. At maturity, a Pygmy Griffin weighs about 100kg and has golden brown feathers while its full-sized cousin can weigh upward of 300kg, with white feathers. Unlike the Chimera, Griffins are generally placid and can be approached. However, when caring for young, the female Griffin becomes very territorial and has been known to attack humans.

Grootslang—A giant serpent with the trunk and head of an elephant. The Grootslang lives in marshy areas and prefers to spend most of its time in the water. It is known to hunt young elephants by making a trumpeting noise, reminiscent of their herd, which lures the unsuspecting creature into the water. The Grootslang is nonvenomous and constricts in the manner of a python to strangle its prey. Unmounted human beings can generally approach in relative safety, as the Grootslang views them as too small to be prey.

Hogfish—Also known as the Ambize. Closely related to the Sea-Swine, found Northern oceans. The hogfish is a lake-dwelling creature that has the head of a pig with the body of a fish, and hominoid style hands. Despite its gruesome appearance, the Hogfish is a vegetarian and feeds on algae and seaweed.

Hydra—A rare three-headed reptile that lives in lakes, oceans, and rivers. Contrary to myth, the Hydra is not a dragon nor very large. Most mature Hydra grow only to the size of a large dog and cannot pose a threat to humans. Its heads are known to argue for food, and as a result, many Hydra often die from the competition. Hydra have the keenest sense of smell in the animal kingdom—more accurate even than sharks or bloodhounds. These predators can smell a single drop of blood in the water from over two miles away.

Morgawr—A fifteen-ton sea creature with razor sharp teeth and a long, giraffish neck. Many people are put off by the Morgawr's fearsome appearance, but it is in fact a close relative of the Echalend manatee. Its teeth allow it to feed on whole trees, easily grinding the wood into a pulp. The Morgawr is so gentle that native people in Nazwimbe record stories of using it as a ferryboat at river crossings. Morgawr cud is highly prized and many hunters seek out these docile creatures to collect the wood cud that drips from their mouth to make paper.

Nkombe—A brilliant gold bird, famed as the savior of the sun in mythology. The Nkombe flies higher than any other bird, and is said to greet the sun each morning when it wakes. As a result of conservational efforts by the government, the Nkombe's feathers are often used in chieftain's headdresses in place of the more traditional Caladrius feathers.

Phoenix—Although it's a beautiful animal with striking gold, red, orange, and yellow feathers, the Phoenix is closely related to the common pigeon. Many visitors from Echalend actively seek the Phoenix on arrival to Nazwimbe, much to the bemusement of the locals. The Phoenix has a beautiful song and is a confident, showy bird that will often reveal itself to people.

River Mermaid—An amphibious species with a hominoid upper body and the tail of a fish. Two species of mermaid exist globally, but the ocean mermaid does not live in the warm Nazwimbe waters. Unlike its solitary ocean cousin, the river mermaid travels in large schools. The mermaid can be safely approached while the viewer is on land, but beware, mermaids attack in groups and have been known to strip a carcass faster than a school of piranha.

White Unicorn—*Unicornalis Kardunn*—the famous White Unicorn of Nazwimbe. Although equine in appearance, the Unicorn has a long ivory horn that grows throughout its lifetime. As it ages, the Unicorn's horn develops silver spirals. It lives a solitary life, other than when mating. The Unicorn is unique among animals in that it can choose when to end its own gestation period. Despite its equine-like body, the unicorn possesses a much higher level of intelligence and strength. It can only be domesticated if raised from birth, and even then, it will only accept a rider by choice. Unscrupulous humans have determined that by removing the Unicorn's horn, it can be enslaved. However, if enslaved in this manner, the unicorn will die within a year.

Acknowledgments

THIS BOOK would not be possible without the extensive support and work of many people in my life:

To Dad: So much of what inspires me to write comes from the places you've taken me. Your wanderlust and curiosity about the world is inspiring, and I have so many amazing memories from the trips we went on. I will always remember stalking a pair of leopards at night at Mala Mala, flying in an air balloon over Bagan, snorkeling over the clams in Australia, the doubling game and the dinner-time geography quizzes. All those memories and experiences make the worlds I imagine in my writing so much richer.

To Mom: They say that to be able to write well, you have to be a reader first. You nurtured my love of books right from the get-go. I still remember sitting in my room with you, while you read books like *Owls in the Family* and *The Great Brain*. I never knew your secret plan to get me to read more until I was much older, but it definitely made a difference. Even now, when I'm twenty-six, we're still reading books together.

To Tamara, KT, Elisabeth and Naomi: Thank you for battling through this book when it was in its earliest stages and for giving me such useful feedback. This book is much better because of your work. KT, you have supported me at every stage of the publishing process. You've become an amazing friend and my virtual shoulder to cry, rage and fret on.

To Cam, Rue, Zan, Erin, Jenny and the rest of my Edinburgh-based family by choice: Thank you for being so supportive of me when I was going through a genuinely rough time, and for getting so excited with me at the announcement of this book's publication!

To Megan Moss, my amazing cover artist: You created a cover that is truly a work of art in itself. Your renderings perfectly capture the girls as I always imagined them. Thank you!

To Dawn, my senior editor at Harmony Ink: This manuscript took a bit of patience and perseverance on your part! I remain amazed at your attention to detail and ability to remember so many things about the book at once! Sorry about all the comma splices! Thanks to your hard work, I'm feeling so much more confident about letting this book go out into the world.

To the amazing team at Harmony Ink: Thank you for all your amazing work on the book, and always answering all my questions so promptly. You've been an amazing publisher to work with, and I've met so many supportive authors in the community through you (special shout out to Nina Rossing!).

Originally from Chicago, JULIA EMBER now resides in sunny Scotland, where she has learned to enjoy both haggis and black pudding. She spends her days working as a professional Book Nerd and her nights writing YA Romantic Fantasy novels. She also spends an inordinate amount of time managing her growing city-based menagerie of pets with Harry Potter–themed names. Presently, she is the haggard slave of the cats Sirius Black and Luna Lovegood and Bellatrix Le Snake. A lifelong horse-lover, she also owns a freakishly adorable cob pony called Africa. Her animals tend to make cameo appearances in her writing.

A world traveler since childhood, Julia has now visited over sixty countries. Her travels inspire the fictional worlds she writes about, and she populates those worlds with magic and monsters.

When she isn't working or writing, Julia enjoys exploring the magical city of Edinburgh, riding horses, reading too many books, and trying out new restaurants!

Readers can contact Julia via her website: www.julia-ember.com
Or connect with her through Twitter: @jules_chronicle

GUÐSRIKI

ARI BACH

www.harmonyinkpress.com

SARA GAINES

NOBLE
FALLING

www.harmonyinkpress.com

Pretty Peg

Skye Allen

Zoe Lynne

That Witch!

www.harmonyinkpress.com

CPSIA information can be obtained
at www.ICGtesting.com
Printed in the USA
FSOW04n2026110816
23699FS